MERCER
UNIVERSITY PRESS

Endowed by
TOM WATSON BROWN
and
THE WATSON-BROWN FOUNDATION, INC.

Whiskey before Breakfast

A Novel

Benjy Griffith

Mercer University Press
Macon, Georgia

MUP/H766

© 2008 Mercer University Press
1400 Coleman Avenue
Macon, Georgia 31207
All rights reserved

First Edition.

Books published by Mercer University Press are printed on acid free
paper that meets the requirements of American National Standard for
Information Sciences—Permanence of Paper for Printed Library
Materials.

Mercer University Press is a member of Green Press initiative
(greenpressinitiative.org), a nonprofit organization working to help
publishers and printers increase their use of recycled paper and decrease
their use of fiber derived from endangered forests. This book is printed
on recycled paper.

Library of Congress Cataloging-in-Publication Data

978-0-088146-123-7

    Griffith, Benjy.
    Whiskey before breakfast : a novel / Benjy Griffith. -- 1st edition.
    p. cm.
    ISBN-13: 978-0-88146-123-7 (hardback : alk. paper)
    ISBN-10: 0-88146-123-7 (hardback : alk. paper)
    1. Georgia—History—20th century—Fiction.
2. Depressions—1929—United States—Fiction. 3. Domestic fiction.
I. Title.
    PS3607.R5485W44 2008
    813'.6—dc22
                                                              2008030506

For their love and support, I dedicate this novel to my parents, my wife Teresa, my sister Eugenia, and my children: Wes, Casey, Travis, and Jessica

Acknowledgments

I am especially grateful to Peggy Chastain for typing multiple versions of this novel, to my father for his careful reading of the various drafts and his constant encouragement, and to Shannon Ravenal for her editing expertise, to Bill Larsen for his help with legal terms and the courtroom scene, and to my friends in Juliette, Georgia, especially Marvin Bowdoin, whose store was the hangout for many colorful characters.

Whiskey before Breakfast

CHAPTER 1

The Indians said the shad used to spawn so thick in this river you could walk across the water on their backs. But the shad no longer spawn in this river, and the old fields and ceremonial mounds that rise out of the flatlands a few miles downstream moan with the dead of twelve thousand years.

At first the settlers came in small measure. But soon they descended like the drone of locust: the endless clatter and drawl of rough-bearded, mule-drawn men who snarled their irreverence in passing as they spit tobacco off the side of buckboards and re-snapped the reins, circumnavigating these burial mounds to stake a patch of good bottom land, then girdle the landscape like mad beavers gnawing out of the swamps.

The first drove came with a Bible clutched in the left hand and a corn whiskey jug dangling from the right, dragging the African along to clear the old-growth forests and scatter the hard black cotton seeds to rise among the dead stumps. And sometimes late at night, the drums would sound, echoing down the river like lost wildebeest striding, lions backtracking, toward some distant land.

Soon the fields stretched farther south than the horizon itself until one copper autumn the sons and grandsons of these same men turned north, now gray-coated soldiers fit with musket, marching out the roads of the countryside. Then, one April dawn, he appeared on a sorrel thoroughbred gelding, the bearded general with insistent hazel eyes. And for days and nights the earth itself seemed to shatter against the sky, a thousand fires spitting toward the stars until he too left, his task complete.

The years that followed were as fallow as the weed-choked land itself until once again they came, returning to reconfigure the fields and deepen the plows. Only this time the whites and Africans were hitched together like a mule-trader's string of culls, thin-ribbed and hollow-eyed; the gaunt white, still hard-mouthed and headstrong, holding the lead mule position where he could foul the occasional sweet whiff of freedom from the African, not with the mustiness of his own liquored sweat, but now with a cotton hood to mask his face.

Soon the endless cotton field gave way to the pine timber that twisted out of the spent soil to crop another breed, men who bargained with whiskey and pistols to take the land and set up sawmills to buzz like the sudden hatch of mosquitoes moving toward the scent of new blood. Men who came from Virginia and South Carolina and even Pennsylvania, not for the land in and of itself, but bound by the dream of their fathers and even their Scotch and Irish ancestors before them: to satisfy an entire lineage of hunger and want until their bellies were full and hard on it. They were men like Earl Ham from Redbone, Georgia, who drove a Ford truck this October morning in 1937 before dawn had begun to grey the sky. His son, Newt, stared out the window, letting the broad darkness outside the truck dull his senses as he waited for the mood of his father to surface; he didn't dare speak until he knew it. He had heard his father pacing the hall the night before, had heard the guttural bellows of discontent, the "quit your goddamned bawling and moping 'round here woman," and finally the cold ring of thick glass and whiskey bottle rattling out of the cabinet, all indistinguishable from a dream now. When the door cracked with the widening slither of light, the boy had risen without a word and followed his father down the hall. He passed the dark bedroom where his mother sat in a white gown on the edge of the bed, hands clasped. She did not look up from her hands as he passed down the hall.

When Earl Ham finally cleared his throat to speak, it rumbled from deep within, forcing the air to boil up from his throat and roil in his jowls as if it were some meaty contraption that was controlled by the half-chewed cigar in his teeth. "How old you say you was, boy?"

"Thirteen, Papa."

Earl Ham cleared his throat again, swallowed hard. "Thirteen? Goddamn boy. Time I was thirteen I was making me a living running four mules and a logging crew for Papa. Had me plenty of young gals. Shit. Women, too, 'fore I was your age. You can bet your little ass your papa had 'em. Never made no difference to me what color they was long as I had a mess of 'em." He leaned over and nudged his shoulder into the boy without taking his eye off the road. "How much of that old poontang you done had you, boy?" Earl jabbed his elbow in Newt's rib cage. "'Fess up now, boy. Make your old papa proud."

Newt looked up from his lap toward his father and watched him laugh freely from his chest, a raspy, unsettling laugh that sharpened the boy's senses. Newt's blond hair hung loose over his forehead, and his green eyes, at once innocent and intuitive, peered out from beneath the rim of his grandfather's old felt fedora as if he were somehow drawing the light off the object he was looking at to sparkle in his own eyes. The boy had that rare gentleness of cheek leading into the eyes that attracted stray dogs and strangers, and one day, no doubt, would be desired by women, too. The boy's voice, as well, held an affable quality, a graciousness when he spoke: "What kind of mules did Granddaddy have back then, Papa? Were they them big old Belgian bred mules or just them small ones like most folks 'round here got?"

Earl cut his eyes over to the boy, looked down his nose and cigar, and lightly growled, irritated that Newt had soft-stepped his question. "Boy, let me tell you something you been needing to hear. You ain't doing a damn thing but wasting time fooling round with that slobbering-ass brother of yours."

Newt took a deep but silent breath before he spoke again. "It looks to me like Addie's getting better all the time, Papa. Just yesterday he helped me load all them feed sacks in the barn. He's strong, Papa. Real strong. He can do good work if somebody'll just show him what to do and how to do it. Mama says if you look real hard, you can see God in his eyes."

"God? God, my ass. Ain't no goddamned God in that young 'un. Where you reckon this here God was when He made him, napping on some fluffy-ass cloud somewheres thinking, 'I'll just make me a goddamned idiot come sunrise?'" Earl shook his head emphatically. "That boy won't never 'mount to nothing. Let the women folks tend to him. You ain't got no business messing 'round with him all the time. They's more important things for you to be tending to, boy."

Earl hunched forward and squinted down the road, squeezing the steering wheel with both hands until his knuckles whitened. Then he relaxed back down in his seat and struck a match against the dash to finally light his cigar. He blew the match cold without taking the cigar from his mouth. "Now look here, boy. I done had my eye on that moonshine business up the river at Berner for a long time now. Too goddamned long's what I say. Well, by God, I woke up last night and I said to myself, 'Earl, ain't no chicken shit son of a bitch like Sonny Tuggle gonna keep you out of taking what's rightly yours.' So I done struck me up a plan, son."

Earl waved his cigar loosely toward the boy as his voice took on a more sober tone. "Listen up real close here to what your papa's fixing to lay out. You know that hand of mine they call Jefferson, don't you boy?"

"Yes sir, Papa. He's the one that they always talking 'bout that's so good with a crosscut saw, ain't he?"

"Yeah, that's him. Stays good and goddamned drunk from payday through Sunday's what he's good at. Well, come to find out he got his self a cousin they call Isaac that lives up on Sonny Tuggle's place, works in his sawmill too." Earl flipped the back of his hand into Newt's chest to accent the point. "That's how we'll cut in on Tuggle's whiskey business, boy.

"I'll tell Jefferson to send for Isaac, telling him that their granny is sick or something, done sent for to see him. Now when Isaac gets down here we'll tell him 'bout our plan to sell 'shine up his way. We'll cut him in enough to keep him interested. Then we'll send Jefferson up to Berner along with Isaac with a full load of whiskey. Isaac can go on into Tuggle's mill that Friday afternoon 'bout quitting time and tell all them folks that his cousin's done showed up with the finest corn liquor ever been made on Sweetwater Branch, and it's fifty cent a quart cheaper than what they been paying. You hear me, boy?"

"Yes sir, Papa. I hear you."

"Then y'all gonna meet all them folks down at Isaac's house come quitting time and sell four cases to 'em. We'll give Jefferson a gallon for every four cases he sells. He'll sell it too, by God. A whiskey buyer believes a whiskey drinker. You remember that, boy."

"I will, Papa."

Earl sucked the cigar back to a red coal, then puffed a white cloud of smoke. A hint of a smile curled from the corner of his mouth. "There won't be no stopping us then, boy. Once they get a taste of Beaucat's whiskey there won't be no such a thing as

Sonny Tuggle's whiskey business no more. It'll dry up like his poor-ass cotton crop done."

Newt looked over at Earl to make certain he had finished speaking. "You said *y'all* like you was including me in on it, Papa."

Earl turned quickly on the boy. "Hell yeah, *y'all*. You heard it right, boy. Y'all's where in the hell you come in. I'm sending your ass up there with Jefferson to look after the money. You do know how to add up things in your head, don't you, boy?"

"Yes sir, I can add."

"I got me a money belt to strap on you 'fore you leave out. You know how to shoot a pistol don't you, boy?"

"I've hit some bottles with one before," Newt said.

"Good. Now don't let them two get drunk as all hell and trade that whiskey for no woman. Or sell none on credit neither. Bring back all cash. You with me, boy?"

Newt sat up in the seat, stretching to look out the window at the horizon where dawn had begun to break over the fields. He had heard the stories about the village of Berner, the shootings and knifings and even the stories of the gambling and wild women, and although he had expected fear to rise within him, it had not. He took in a deep breath of the crisp morning air and looked straight ahead, reconciling himself to every twist in the road as it came upon him, allowing the silence itself to answer his father's question.

CHAPTER 2

A stiff slug of whiskey before breakfast is how Jefferson started every Saturday morning. Then he'd saddle his mule and head to Mr. Bludie's store, his liquor tucked in his overalls. They always said you could hear him coming from where Third Branch Creek crosses Barron Russell Road with his fast but measured liquor mouth preaching from the saddle to every hedgerow thicket and fencepost along the way—that hard liquor mouth ringing closer and closer, the way a good coon dog bays every breath as it pushes a hot track up the creek and finally trees in the hackberry by your barn. He could feel the liquor moving in him good now, the way only liquor on an empty stomach moves evenly and with purpose.

Jefferson always made sure to gather himself up and sit tall in the saddle when he got in sight of the store. He rode in an old World War I cavalry saddle his father left him, and he kept it clean. His long legs made the stirrups hang low on Emma, and his back was straight, rising up to the red bandana around his neck. He pulled the felt hat low over his eyes so that it pointed just over the mule's ears, then clucked to Emma through a closed mouth, putting her in a fancy flat walk through the crossroads: "Show up in here, gal. Lord have mercy. That's what I'm talking 'bout."

Then he started in on the three men slouching on the store bench, full throttle, like a brush-arbor preacher busting out of the thicket. "Great godalmighty and the Ship of Zion. Y'all best be getting ready peoples. That's right. I knows what I'm talking 'bout. This man you looking at done cut and stacked fourteen loads of wood this week. Ain't nobody to help me but this here mule I'm setting on. Shit. One man can't stand me all day on that crosscut saw. Hell naw. Th-th-that mule boss say 'slow down boy you gwine work that mule to the ground.' Lord knows I was getting down."

Jefferson dismounted and stood for a moment with the reins in his hands, not looking at the rolling hills or the graying sky, but at that place where ground and sky meet, as if trying to judge the distance of the horizon. He led the mule around to the side of the store, letting the gravel shuffle of her hooves do the talking now. He tethered the mule to a rail, loosened her girth, and took one long pull from the pint bottle before pushing it deep in his saddlebag.

Jefferson walked past the three men on the bench and stopped to brush the slick faded knees of his overalls. "Y'all better listen at what I'm telling you. When that great godalmighty ship come, or when this here man standing in front of y'all and that mule come loping 'cross them crossroads, y'all swear 'fore God better be ready then. Believe what I'm telling you now. Just be ready."

They sat and said nothing, never looking him in the eye but seeing the whole of him as he passed in front of them and stopped. They listened to his words not with respect but with the same unspoken reverence you give a yapping feist at the end of a stranger's porch, not afraid to turn and hush him up, but too wise to do so, knowing that sooner or later he will move from the porch to under the house and scratch in the cool yellow dirt, curl up, and be silent.

Jefferson opened the screen door and walked down a narrow side aisle of the store that was walled with canned goods and cluttered with plow blades, hoes, and coiled plow line. Before he stopped he felt across his front pocket to make sure he had left the pint behind. Mr. Bludie's back was toward him at the meat counter, the white apron double folded and bloody, high on his waist, the meat ax moving short then long over a slab of ribs. The ax quit moving as he looked around his shoulder and over his glasses toward Jefferson. He looked over the rims the way a man looks when he goes from reading something in his lap to squinting into a long distance, and he went back to chopping the meat as if maybe he had not turned around far enough to see Jefferson at all.

Jefferson moved closer. "That sugar done come, Mr. Bludie? Mr. Earl say he want that sugar 'fore noon."

Mr. Bludie took off his glasses and rubbed his eyes with his thumb and forefinger. "Well, let me tell you what you do then. Why don't you just take that Emma mule and head on up the tracks and tell 'em what a powerful hurry y'all is in to see Mr. Earl's sugar."

Jefferson tugged the brim of his hat closer to his eyes. "Alls I know is Mr. Earl say he want his sugar 'fore noon."

Mr. Bludie resumed his meat chopping and then stopped abruptly, pointing the ax northward up the tracks. "Let me tell you a little something about the sugar business you might not a knowed. That's Dixie's sugar on that railroad; it's my sugar when they set that car off the rail. It ain't Mr. Earl's sugar till him and his boys load their wagons and sign up that bill. Then it's Mr. Earl's sugar." Mr. Bludie hacked the slab of ribs in two, then stopped again, this time pointing the meat ax directly at Jefferson. "But that ain't all. Cause 'fore long it'll be y'all's sugar tit to suck out them bottles. Then it won't be Mr. Earl's sugar no more at all, it'll be a dollar and a quarter sugar tit, and then Saturday night spine and who'll cut who, and six bottles by Sunday evening'll be seven dollars and a half and no grocery money on Wednesday, only Mr. Earl's pocket picking y'all's bones clean as a buzzard picking a dead coon in the ditch side the road."

There was a long pause as Jefferson tried blankly to digest the onslaught of words. "Yes sir," he said, with neither presumption nor deference, then turned and walked back down the aisle and out the screen door, not stopping until he got to the mule and the saddlebags and the bottle and drank two long pulls before putting it back in his overalls. He walked back to the front porch of the store and squatted down by the crates in the corner, his arms around his knees and his back leaning against the wall, warm again as he looked up at the gray October sky.

Jefferson dug a square of tobacco out of his pocket and cut a wedge off with his knife, moving the tobacco and blade toward his outstretched lips. He folded the knife against his hip and slid it into his pocket in one motion. After working the tobacco down deep in his jaw, he spat over his left shoulder and stood up, leaning against the wall. "Who done seen Mr. Earl this morning?"

The men on the bench said nothing.

Jefferson pulled a sassafras stem from his front overalls pocket and stuck it in his front teeth, giving it a sharp sucking sound before he spoke again. "Don't make me come over there with this hawkbill in my pocket. I done got it open. It ain't nothing for me to cut a man on Saturday morning. I done done it plenty a times. I'll cut some black asses Saturday morning red."

Mudcat stood up from the bench. "You don't scare nobody 'round here. Mr. Bludie hear you talking all that shit out here this morning you know what he gone do."

"Shit. What he gone do?" Jefferson asked. "Whup me with his meat rag? Lord knows I ain't telling no lie. Ain't no white man gone put his hand on me. That's right. You better believes that."

Mudcat cocked his hat a few degrees to the right. "Don't nobody 'round here care about hearing all your shit."

Jefferson took a step forward and half stumbled, keeping his knee bent as if he felt the earth shift slightly beneath him, but he managed to narrow his eyes down to fine slits, daring Mudcat to continue.

"That's right. You heard me." Mudcat shuffled slowly backwards with his hands in his pockets and bobbed his head up and down as if he had suddenly found his rhythm. "Yes sir. Like Mr. Bludie done said. Ain't much of your black ass Mr. Earl don't own."

Jefferson looked over Mudcat's shoulder into the gray sky, unable to focus on the words being spoken or even the face beneath the cap, finally releasing even the sounds themselves from his grasp the way the last cold ring of a church bell loses its own sound to the horizon.

Jefferson was back on the dirt road now with the bottle in his hand, his arms crossed out over the saddle horn, the head and felt hat bobbing in the space between the mule's neck and the horn. The mule walked slowly, stopping now and then to shoulder the weight back into place before taking the next step. Emma walked off the road and down the trail toward the old Benham homeplace, through the privet hedge past the old falling chimney, and stopped. Jefferson slid down out of the rhythm that was not rhythm now, but just his movement out of the saddle and onto the ground like the sliding fall through a window onto the floor. There he lay while the mule nibbled the wild rye of the homeplace yard in between the jonquils and fallen bricks. She worked the edges of the hedgerows for the most tender grass, every now and then blowing from her nostrils, the soft natural blow of being satisfied.

The mule stopped eating and stood still with only her tail moving against the flies, watching over the black arms and red shirt motionless in the green grass with the sky getting darker, the shades of gray heavier, waiting for the turn of an elbow from the arm or the raising of a knee from the overalls.

Emma's ears stood straight up when she saw Ida coming. The mule turned just her head and not her body, following the figure moving up the road until she began to recognize the gait of the person, and then the familiar red bandana on her head, and then the hands behind her back as she walked toward them with her eyes fixed on the ground ahead of her feet, never looking at the mule, but knowing Emma would be there and him, too, in the grass.

Ida walked past the mule, gathered the reins in her hand, and bent over Jefferson, saying nothing at first, just looking down at the body, not with disgust or even sympathy but as if looking over a basket of laundry. Then she put her hand on his shoulder and firmly shook. "Jefferson...Jefferson...Get on up now. It's time to get on home."

CHAPTER 3

By noon Friday, Jefferson and Isaac had loaded the floorboard of the pulpwood truck with four cases of whiskey and were on their way to Earl Ham's house to pick up Newt. Newt's mother sat at a desk by the front window where she creased the letter she had written and folded it into an envelope. She printed the address with a deliberate precision. As she looked out the window she caught a reflection of herself in the glass pane, and she turned her chin down, as if struggling to recognize the woman who was framed there. She had never liked Georgia as much as her home in South Carolina. She missed the low country, its lush marshes and cypress-stained rivers, and had never grown accustomed to the red clay hills or the muddy river running through them.

She pulled her blond hair back tight and re-knotted it. Standing up, she slid the letter into her apron pocket and squinted through her own image to watch Newt and his younger brother chase a game hen around the yard. The younger boy was clapping his hands and laughing as Newt dove under the front porch and came back out holding the chicken by its leg, upside down and flapping. When Newt saw the truck, he tossed the chicken in the air and grabbed the boy's hand. Leading him up on the front porch, Newt called to his mama through the screen door.

She came through the door glaring at the truck, knowing that the eyes inside of it would not dare meet hers but once. She put her arm around the younger boy and gave Newt a hug on her other side, then straightened her shoulders to face the truck again. Newt patted his open hand gently on his brother's cheek, and the younger boy rolled his knuckles across his forehead and put two fingers in his mouth. Carrying a small burlap bag tied with a knot,

Newt trotted to the truck and hopped into the front seat. "We better hurry," he said.

As the truck left the yard, Newt's brother struggled to free himself from his mama. She crouched to her knees and pulled him closer, but he fought through her arms, finally pulling free as the truck left the driveway and entered the road. Jefferson and Newt turned to look through the back windshield as the boy came hard after them, his stiff-legged gait stirring the dust red, arms pumping, red tongue thick and to the side until the feet and the legs finally disappeared from under him. He rolled onto his back, then raised his head off the ground to watch the truck disappear through the trees. He put the two fingers into his mouth again and let his head fall back the ground.

"Doggonnit," Newt said. "I should of knowed she couldn't hold him back."

"What's wrong with that boy?" Isaac asked.

"Aw, he's just retarded," Newt said. "He's a good brother, though. But he ain't never said a word in his life that anybody could understand. He ain't even ever said mama or papa. Mama's always saying you can see God in him if you look real hard. Mama says he's special, like Lazarus in the Bible, cause they say he was dead, wasn't breathing at all when he come out. The doctor put the sheet over his head and everything and that's when he started squalling. His real name's Adam. We all call him Addie except for Papa. Only thing he calls him by is 'that boy.'"

Isaac glanced out the back window. "He don't run too good, do he?"

"Aw, he can run pretty fast when I'm running right beside him. He was more throwing a fit back there than really running 'cause I didn't take him with us."

Isaac nodded his understanding.

Newt took a deep breath before continuing, "The preacher from Mama's church came by one evening to talk about baptizing him, and he told Mama that Addie had been touched by the hand of the Lord and that we ought to be able to see a reflection of our soul in him. I looked at him real hard every day after that, trying to see the reflection of that soul the preacher was talking about, but I can't say I ever did see it.

"But I do think Mama was right about God being in there 'cause one night when we were laid on our backs in the grass looking at the stars, all of a sudden a long shooting star came over and Addie made this sound like an angel moaning or something, and I got up on my knees and looked into his eyes. I can't swear to it or nothing, but I'm almost sure I saw God then."

Jefferson looked over to Newt and shifted the truck's gear down abruptly as if to stagger the momentum of the boy's words. Newt lunged slightly forward but caught himself on the dash, then started up again before he sat all the way back in his seat.

"Papa said he don't think he can make a man out of him, though. He wants to send him off somewheres, but Mama said if he went she was going too, and Papa ain't said nothing else about it.

"Addie wants a puppy real bad, but Papa won't let him have one. One day a little old stray yellow pup wandered up to the house, and we kept him hid in the barn for a week. Addie'd be down there all day holding that pup, rubbing his head, smelling his breath. I swear, I ain't never seen nobody that liked to smell puppy breath as much as he does. But Papa found out about it and took the pup off up the road, and a little while later I heard a shot, but Addie didn't know what it was. I'm planning on saving up my money to buy him a real nice pup one day. I figure if I get a real nice hound pup that'll hunt for Papa, then maybe he won't shoot it. Addie's just retarded, that's all."

Jefferson looked down at the boy when he had finished talking as if he was looking at some strange varmint he had never seen in the woods before. Then he put the sassafras twig in his mouth and gave it a sharp suck with his lips parted. He spoke slowly and deliberately, as if to afford the boy the pleasure of hearing every word. "Lord help us if you's set on talking that much all the time, boy."

"Naw, I ain't. Sometimes I just sit and think about things and watch stuff."

"What all's in that sack?" Isaac asked.

"Two chicken sandwiches and a biscuit and a pair of drawers and socks and a shirt. But you ain't got to worry. They ain't all together. Mama got them sandwiches and that biscuit wrapped up in a paper bag and them drawers is clean anyway. We can split one of them sandwiches and that biscuit if y'all's hungry. I don't care. I'd like to save one for tonight, but if y'all's real hungry we can eat it, too."

Newt unfolded the knot and pulled a sandwich from the bag, giving half to Isaac and half to Jefferson, and broke the biscuit into three parts, keeping one and giving them the rest.

Jefferson drove them down the river road, with the liquor under their feet and the windows open, past the fennel-choked cotton patches and through the wood smoke of old chimneyed shacks tilted off the sides of hills. They passed Tarentine's Ferry at Tom's Crossing and stopped to let a wagon pulled by two sorrel mules swing wide. An old black man with a gray beard and pointed straw hat shook the reins on the mules' backs and moved them into line behind the other wagons waiting to load onto the ferry.

"We gwine make it before quitting time?" Jefferson asked.

"What time it be?" Isaac asked.

They turned to the boy, who looked out into the sky through the front windshield. Then they all looked up through the windshield and tried to find the sun in the sky.

"It ain't far off two o'clock," the boy said.

Isaac shifted impatiently in his seat, rocking gently forward and back as he looked out the front and then the back of the truck. He rubbed his thighs as if they were cold. "Mr. Sonny catch me selling Mr. Earl's whiskey up here, ain't no telling what he liable to do."

Jefferson tilted his head back and squinted down the road. "What difference it make who you working for, long as you making money?"

"What difference it make?" Isaac repeated. "You coming up here working for your boss man. And here I is working against mine. And mine a good man too—for a white man. He treat his peoples good. I ain't lying. Sends the Doc over to the women folks when they has they babies. He even give 'em a five-dollar gold piece when the baby come. Yes sir. That what Mr. Sonny Tuggle do."

Isaac quit rocking and sat up straight. "Mr. Sonny don't allow no foolishness though. Ain't no use to get him riled. One time the sheriff locked him up a man named Wash what worked for Mr. Sonny. They was all saying this and that 'bout him and a white woman, but Wash, he say he just minding his own business walking down the street, didn't do no more'n look in the door of that dress store. But they took him on to the jailhouse just the same.

"Well sir, Mr. Sonny Tuggle he rode that big bay gelding of his'n, Dusty they called that big old hoss, head way up high, rode him on down the main road to town and right up them stairs of that courthouse and all the way inside. And he don't even get off that hoss. He just setting on his back hollering, 'Hey. Y'all turn my man loose. I need him in the fields.' That's just what he said now. They let him go that minute, too. Ain't been back neither. No sir. Ain't been back. That's the God's truth there now. You ask anybody 'round here. They'll tell you."

"Dang," Newt said. "I sure would be proud of my papa if he done something like that."

Jefferson gave the boy a curious sidling glance. "You ain't got to worry none 'bout that. Now get me out one of them whiskey bottles so's I can take me a drink."

"Naw," Isaac said. "Don't pull out that whiskey 'round here."

Jefferson gave Isaac a hard look, but Isaac kept on rubbing his thighs, looking down the road.

When they arrived at the mill, Jefferson turned down a small trail that led him to the side of the building and parked out of sight from the road.

"Y'all go on down to my house and wait for me there," Isaac said. "I'm fixing to get my pay and do what Mr. Earl say do. I'll be on down to the house 'fore it get dark."

Jefferson turned the truck around and headed toward Isaac's shack. He steered carefully through the village, taking time to look through his window at the people on the front porches and gathered in twos or threes under shade trees in the hard-packed dirt yards. Their eyes turned away from the truck as it got closer. They gave no wave, no nod at its approach.

The boy looked out the same side of the truck but was not watching the people or the porches, only Jefferson, comparing the color of his skin to the color of coffee in the morning light being poured out of the spout and into a cup, looking at his short-brimmed felt hat pushed to the back of his head, giving full light to the angular forehead and broad nose. When relaxed, Jefferson kept his full lips slightly parted, able to quickly force a thin smile if he had to, but mostly he kept the weathered lips tight and pointed forward, working a sassafras twig in all possible angles above the muscled jaw. Newt studied Jefferson's eyes the longest. They were close-set and the color of a shelled pecan, but with a hint of yellow when the sun hit them; the eyelids were fleshy and sometimes lazy, partially covering his eyes and giving him the slightest hint of an oriental look. His gaze reminded the boy of one of his mama's game hens, a gaze that you could never really read until it finally turned and focused on you alone.

Jefferson turned on the boy. "What you looking at?"

"I was just looking to see if I could figure out how old you was," Newt said.

Jefferson pursed his lip. "How come you ain't at the schoolhouse?"

"'Cause of Papa. He said it's time I started learning something about the business. I'd a heap rather be out here riding with y'all than being at school playing marbles at recess anyhow. I wouldn't mind missing every Friday. That way at least I'll get a little break from that girl at school that keeps on chasing me. Mary Beth Franks. That's her name. She wears glasses. One day she done it, too. Caught me coming around the corner of the schoolhouse and laid one right on my mouth 'fore I even knew what was happening. Now I have to peep every corner I go around."

Jefferson glanced in the rearview mirror and then sped up a little.

"How many young 'uns you and Miss Ida got anyhow?" Newt asked.

"Who says we got 'em?" Jefferson snapped back.

"How come? Miss Ida don't want no young 'uns? That'd be hard to believe. I like Miss Ida. She does Mama's sewing sometimes, and I listen to her and Mama talking in the kitchen.

She knows a lot about the Bible, don't she? Goodness gracious
alive. Mama said she can sing real good, too. Mama says she loves
that song bout the Ship of Zion. They don't make 'em no better'n
Miss Ida, Mama says."

"She all right," Jefferson said as he pulled off the road at
Isaac's shack and angled the truck toward the back door.

"We just sit here till Isaac come," Jefferson said.

"I ain't in no hurry. I like to travel. I like meeting new people.
Some things up here look better than they do at home, don't they,
Jefferson? They ain't as much old stuff laying up on the side of the
road and in peoples' yards and things. I always heard it was some
kind of rough up here, but it probably ain't as bad as everybody
says. They's bound to be some nice folks up here."

Jefferson fidgeted in his seat as the boy spoke, then moved
the floor mat to the side and pulled out a bottle. He took only a
taste the first time; his cheeks rippled like he had bitten into a
green persimmon. Then he took a long pull and made no face at
all, placing the bottle in his crotch and rolling the cap between his
forefinger and thumb.

CHAPTER 4

Isaac's shack buzzed with the business of payday and whiskey. Jefferson stood over the open cases of liquor, Newt sat on a chair behind him, and Isaac huddled with three men by the wood stove in the kitchen. Isaac and Jefferson brought the money to the boy, who counted it down inside the open burlap bag on his lap, keeping up with the total in his head. He now had twenty-two dollars and fifty cents. He kept looking for a place where he could get the cash into the money belt. He first thought of the outhouse he had seen in the backyard, but decided that carrying the bag of money out of the house alone would be too dangerous. He surveyed the room for a small space to crawl into, but there were too many people in the room for him to hide anywhere. Then he studied the cracked door of the bedroom and made a plan; he would go there when it was safe and have Jefferson watch the door while he hid under the bed and transferred the money safely into the belt.

By the time the women arrived, three cases of the whiskey were gone, and the timbre of the room had heightened like the pitch of cicada when dusk touches the river's edge. Newt sat in a corner with his back tight against the wall, his legs crossed and the burlap sack in his lap. Out on the porch he could hear a guitar played bottleneck style, the long whine of a single string followed by a low rough voice. He could not make out the words, but the rambling moan of the melody reminded him of being alone on the riverbank, watching the water float to somewhere he had never been.

A fleshy, round-shouldered woman in a tight lavender dress stood in the kitchen door leaning against the doorjamb. She moved across the room, her thick ankles wobbling in her high-heeled shoes, to stand in front of a man naked to the waist, lying on the couch. His strong black hand worked from the back of her knee up the thigh and disappeared into what Newt could see were white undergarments. His eyes met Newt's as he pulled the woman down, one big thigh to each side as if she were mounting a pony. The man buried his face in her bosom, and she tilted her head back toward the ceiling, laughing over her bright red tongue.

In the far corner, five men crouched around Isaac as he knelt and shook the dice in his hand, eyes closed toward the ceiling. "Help me, Lord Jesus. A six and a three. Preacher in the pulpit." He rolled the dice out of his hand as deftly as he would have spread mustard-green seeds over a freshly plowed garden. They bounced off the corner wall and rolled still. "That's what I'm talking 'bout," he jumped up, pointing toward the dice. "Take all y'all fools' money."

Isaac took the dice in his hand again, shaking them beside his ear. "These here hands knows where to hold a woman, can pick more cotton than you can tote, work a crosscut saw till you holler 'whoa,' and throw more sevens than you can count and roll mo elev—"

"Hey boy." Jefferson stepped back in the room. "You don't know nothing 'bout no crosscut saw. I'll take a crosscut saw and log a sawmill. Me and two other peoples log that whole mill. Shit. One man can't stand with me all day. That's right. You ask anybody. It don't make no difference to me what I's standing in front of. It's coming down. Dat-dat-dat man with them mules say 'slow down, boy, you gwine work these mules to the ground.' Shit. I was getting down."

Jefferson pursed his lips and shook his head with the conviction of a street preacher. "Y'all got some fine womens up here," he said, turning to look at the lavender dress straddling the man on the sofa. "But Lord Almighty knows y'all ain't got nothing like this Sweetwater Creek whiskey." Jefferson held his jar up at eye level. "This here make a man love all night long. Lord have mercy. These womens 'round hear be hollering 'don't got to pay me no dollar.'" Jefferson surveyed once across the room to make sure he had everyone's attention. "Now, come daylight we be long gone down that river road, peoples. Won't be no more this good Sweetwater except where I come from. Y'all be crying and gnashing them teeths come morning bout how sweet that whiskey was last night."

They crowded around Jefferson as he opened the last case. He exchanged the bottles for the dollars and change, then took the fistful of money over to the boy. When Jefferson moved away, the boy found that the man on the sofa was now standing, staring at him. The man's eyes, covered with a light film, narrowed to a fixed, feral stare. Newt tried to smile as he caught the glare, but found he couldn't move the corners of his mouth upward. He was afraid to look away for fear that if he did, the man would sense it the way a wild animal senses his prey's fear before pouncing. The boy mustered what strength he had to look softly into the man's eyes as if trying to calm them, but that seemed to make the eyes even more penetrating and rabid. When Isaac finally called out the numbers on the dice again, the boy seized the opportunity to turn away, and the big man broke down into a deep-throated laugh, his chest heaving until he finally coughed it to a stop. He staggered back to the dice game and glanced at the boy once, shuffling the long pivot of the right side against the short stride of the left.

When Newt awoke, he was looking at the bottom of a frayed gray mattress and rough splintered bed slats. Panicking, he felt for the burlap bag at his side and reached inside, stirring his hand through the bills. He blew a quiet sigh of relief.

The smell hung like a damp blanket around him, and the boy first wondered if it was the smell of his own fear, the fear of those rabid eyes and the bag not being there, but as he looked under the sides of the bed the smell seemed to be seeping into the room along with the gray fragments of morning light. He recognized the smell of man-sweat and then whiskey in the wet, thick air. But there was something more, something that smelled strangely familiar, like stirring beneath a rotten log for earthworms and unleashing a smell of more than the dirt itself, but of the earth giving rise to the animal that had once lived and died there. But this was not the smell of an animal. It was somehow deeply human.

The boy wondered whether he should stay beneath the bed and wait until he heard Jefferson's voice or crawl quietly out and sneak into the woods to move the money from the burlap bag into the money belt. Then he could hide in the woods in sight of the truck and wait for Jefferson to come. He lay perfectly still for a while longer, even holding his breath to see if he could hear any sound of someone stirring or even a car or horse coming down the dirt road. He heard nothing but the sound of labored breathing, straining against the fragments of gray light.

He worked the burlap bag off his stomach and over to his side to try to move the money from the sack into his money belt, but his arms raked against the mattress and slats. Waiting until the breathing found its long and sure rhythm again, he began inching himself feet-first from under the bed. He had everything but his head and the burlap bag out when he felt the pants tighten around one calf while his body slid across the wooden floor. He drew the sack close to his chest, and when he stopped, he was looking not at a man's eyes and a knife, but at eyes over a low-cut blue dress, and the brown thighs opened to him as she crouched, astraddle over his body. He did not recognize her, had not seen her in the house among the other women. She was thin, with high cheekbones and hazel green eyes. Her hair was not the short tight curls of the other women, but fell relaxed down her shoulders. She turned loose his leg and grabbed his pants at the waist, sliding him closer beneath her. Her breath was as hard as kerosene when she spoke. "What we gots here? Some sweet little white meat."

He watched her wet mouth open purplish and wide as she smiled and grabbed his hand, pulling it up between her thighs until the thighs narrowed. There were no white undergarments this time. She pushed his hand harder between the thighs until he could feel the heat and then the dampness. Then she thrust his fingers inside of her and closed her eyes and wet her lips, moving her hips in a smooth, deep rhythm against his hand. "You wants some of this, baby boy? I gives you alls you wants if you open up that money sack and gives some to me."

Newt heard the creaking of the bed and felt the weight of the springs moving at the same time he saw the movement in her eyes. He felt as if he had been asleep in the woods and had awakened to the large shadow of an animal jumping over his body, a boar hog or even a bear. He could not distinguish any feature of the animal, just the mass of it passing over him. He recognized the movement of a thick black forearm flailing downward and then heard the smack of flesh, the blue dress crumpling to fall below the windowsill.

He crawled quickly back under the bed and out the other side toward the light in the cracked door, pushing the bag in front of him. As he rose in the doorway to his two legs and pulled the door open, he felt the blow to his lower back that sent him reeling past the corner where they had thrown dice and onto the floor where the empty whiskey boxes lay.

He now saw the man in the door, cussing him in tones and rhythms too fast for the boy to understand. As the man walked closer, Newt recognized the eyes and short whiskers and now saw the long scar on the muscular chest angling off the collarbone and across the shoulder, the scar even darker somehow than the man's black skin. In the stiff-legged gait Newt had remembered, the man moved closer and pointed his finger toward the boy as he came: "I'm gone get my knife and then I'm gone cut you, boy, for feeling my woman."

"Ain't no boy gone get cut in here this morning."

The boy had neither heard nor seen Jefferson or had even dared hope that he would be there, but when he recognized the familiar voice, he turned and there Jefferson stood in the kitchen door, his overall strap loose, his long left arm hanging by his side, his right hand buried deep in the pocket of his overalls. Jefferson's eyes were red, but more determined, more sure, than the boy had ever seen them before.

"Ain't?" The big man moved a step closer. "Says who?"

"Says this hawkbill open in my pocket."

Out of the sofa and off the floors they rose to the girl's whimpers and the talk of knives. Suddenly the room was full of more eyes, all watching the big man, his short whiskers and heaving chest with the scar.

"Get over here 'hind me, boy," Jefferson said to Newt without taking his eyes off the man. Newt crawled on the floor to Jefferson and stood up behind him, holding the burlap bag in both arms.

Isaac rose off the couch and approached the big man in the door with his arms up to his chest and his palms open, not with confidence, but with the measured tread of a small dog moving low and sideways toward a bigger one. "It's all right, brother man. He's my peoples, brother man, he's my peoples," Isaac kept repeating.

The big man took his eyes off Jefferson and looked back at the girl in the blue dress with her head down on her knees and then back at Isaac and then back at Jefferson, moving his eyes to the boy again. Then he turned his back toward them and limped in measured steps into the bedroom, stopping to reach into the bedcovers. He moved toward the woman on the floor and stood over her, not looking down at her or seeming to acknowledge the whimper at all, but staring out the window. He turned his head then his body toward Jefferson and the boy and walked slowly past Isaac with the heel of his stiff right leg scraping the floor as he came. He stopped in front of Jefferson and relaxed his brow, smoothing his lined face into a smile. "How 'bouts one more bottle of that sweet whiskey 'fore y'all leave out from here? I gots more money."

Then he reached into his pocket and the knife snapped open in his cocked right arm, and he swung hard across Jefferson's left arm that was digging in the pocket by now and knocked him to the floor. The man stood over Jefferson and pointed the hooked blade, carving it in the air toward Jefferson's eyes. "Now I'm gone cut your smart-talking ass to pieces."

It was the sharp click of metal that made the man turn his head away from Jefferson and look at the boy. Newt stood with the open burlap bag at his feet and the small pistol in both hands pointed at the scarred man's head.

"Mister, I ain't never shot at nothing live before. But I do know that if I pull this trigger this here gun's gonna shoot, and it's gonna go where I point it, and I ain't taking it from off your head. Now if you willing to take the chance that I can hold it steady, then I reckon we'll find out soon enough.

"I seen how quick you moved on Jefferson. If you make one step from where you standing, I'm pulling this trigger. You set down on that floor, Mister. Then close that knife shut and throw it to my feet."

The man threw the stiff leg out in front of him and went down on one knee, never taking his eyes off the barrel of the gun and Newt's eyes fixed behind it. He rolled the knife to Newt's feet with the same motion he had used to rolled the dice the night before.

Jefferson rose, picked up the knife, and moved to Newt's side. They backed through the kitchen with Jefferson holding the knife open, turned their backs toward the house, got in the truck, and drove out of the yard and through the village.

"You hurt bad?" Newt asked.

"Naw. He didn't catch me good with that knife."

"I don't know what I'd of done if I hadn't had that pistol. I would've been too scared to jump on him with nothing. I believe I would of just as soon gone up to a rattlesnake and borrowed a rattle."

"I should of gone on and cut him," Jefferson said. "Been done with it."

"You reckon the rest of them folks would of jumped us if you had?" Newt asked.

"Not once they seed his red blood on the floor," Jefferson answered.

"You know that man?" Newt asked.

"He stay here in Berner. Been on the chain gang for the last two years. That how he got that stiff leg."

"What happened?" Newt asked.

"The man broke it for him running," replied Jefferson.

"What was he on the chain gang for?"

"Killing."

"A white man?"

"Naw."

"What's his name?"

"They calls him Red."

"What'd they let him out for?"

"Mr. Tuggle seen to it somehow."

"Why'd he care, Jefferson?"

"They say his mama used to keep Mr. Tuggle's house for him. But she dead now."

"He ain't the one Mr. Tuggle rode in the courthouse after is he?"

"Hell naw."

By the time they reached Tarentine's Ferry, a light rain had begun to fall, settling the boy's excitement into an easy, familiar rhythm.

"I like the rain, Jefferson. I like the way it smells early in the morning. Sometimes when it rains, Addie comes out on the front porch and sits close beside me, just where his shoulder touches mine. He don't squirm around much at all, just sits there with his warm shoulder next to mine. We sit there watching the rain fall out of the sky onto them dusty fields, just watching the way it makes 'em shine. Sometimes I wonder if Addie sees things I ain't even seeing, the way he starts sorrowing like a dove when a light wind rises off the ground and carries them millions of raindrops way out deep into the fields before it lets 'em fall."

He paused for a moment looking out the window, his eyes gentle with the thought. "One time Addie pulled out a hawk feather he must've found somewhere and rubbed it real soft right here where my arm bends, and he never stopped cooing either. I'll never forget how that felt. It was like some kind of magic spell was on me. 'Cause just for that little while, everything in the whole world seemed more peaceful than you could of ever dreamed it to be."

Jefferson watched the light rain bead on the windshield as he steered the truck over the slick clay road.

"I knows a man what got a good hound bitch up round Hillsboro," Jefferson said. "She can tree a coon. Possum, too. They saying she's bred up."

"We'll be down there. We won't be hard to find."

Newt studied Jefferson for a moment, then slid over a few feet closer. "You know that Beaucat fella?"

"I knows him."

"You ever bought whiskey off of him?"

"I asked him once before. But he say he don't sell just one bottle, say he don't want all them folks around."

"You reckon he'd sell you a case?"

"If you gots the money, old Beaucat'll let you have it. It don't make no never mind to him."

CHAPTER 6

Jefferson went to bed before dark that Saturday evening. He had slept hard, and when he awoke his mind was clear and fresh for the first time he could remember on a Sunday morning. His first thought was the bottle of whiskey that he had given Newt, wishing now he had never parted with it. His body felt so alive that it made him crave the whiskey even more than usual. Every Sunday morning for years, he would lie still in bed, pretending to be asleep until Ida opened the door and stood silently there, looking for some movement from his body. He would hear the soft click of the turned knob as she quietly closed the door, and finally the stiff Sunday heels across the porch on her way to church. Then he would rise, go out to the woodpile, and drink from his hidden bottle, freeing the shackled heaviness that weighted his body against the morning. Sunday morning was never the even, vigorous drunk of a Saturday morning; it was the slow, uneven fanning of a stubborn coal.

He heard Ida in the kitchen humming low, working the pots softly to keep from waking him. He lay in bed for a while, thinking about Newt and the bottle of whiskey hidden by the creek, wondering if he would have any trouble finding the boy. His senses quickened to the smell of strong coffee, and he went over in his mind each of the women he had seen at Isaac's the night before. His thoughts settled on the woman in the blue dress, the long thin body slumped and twisted beneath Red's stare.

After putting on his overalls, Jefferson walked into the kitchen. Ida turned her head from the stove and watched him take his chair without his usual sigh. She poured coffee into two tin cups and sat down with him. He studied her black eyes as she

watched the steam rise off her coffee, the eyes so black that the
softness that glowed from them seemed to come from deep within
her. He was proud that she had a different look than the other
women around Redbone. Her cheekbones were well-defined, the
nose not flat and broad, but set high with a slight, noble crook to
it. Her long black hair was pulled back in a bandana, boldly
accentuating the dignity of her face. Jefferson remembered the
story her family told of the Cherokee blood on her mother's side,
how her great-grandmother had been captured on a South
Carolina plantation raid and escaped into Georgia with the child
on her back.

"The hogs is fed," she started, "and I done seen to the
chickens. I'm about to make you some eggs, then I wants you to
go to church with me. Get you some peace with the Lord."

"Who says I got a quarrel with Him," Jefferson said, rubbing
his thighs as if chilled.

"Jefferson," she said, "Lord knows I don't never ask for
nothing. I lets you come and go as you wants to. Come and fetch
you and that mule off the side of the road, and I don't mind none.
But I'm asking you to come with me this morning and I ain't gone
say no more."

Jefferson watched her delicate figure move back over to the
stove. As she stirred the pots, he looked at her thin broad
shoulders, the trim waist. He could not help wondering if it was
his fault they were childless, the imbalance of his wrongs
measured by some hand he could not yet imagine, could not yet
configure.

When they arrived at the church, Jefferson let Ida off at the
front steps and led Emma around to the side of the building,
tethering her to a hitching post. He found a seat in the back pew,
and there he watched Ida come out with the choir in a crimson
robe, worn and faded yet rich against her natural glow. Her eyes

found his as the choir began to sing. Jefferson held the hymnal open even though he could not read the words, mouthing only those he remembered from Ida's singing. He could feel the eyes among the whispers. "She finally got that drunk sonofabitch to church, praise the Lord. Let's see what he gone do. He don't look like he been dranking. His eyes is red though."

The preacher smiled at him from the pulpit as if Jefferson was a promising young hound turned up after being counted for dead or lost. When the choir finally stopped, the preacher placed his hands flat on the pulpit and fixed his smile on Jefferson, tossing his head from side to side in a gracious symmetry as he spoke. "The Lord surely do work in mysterious ways don't he, peoples?"

"Praise the Lord," they shouted.

"Like the song say: Once I was lost, but now I is found. Was blind, Lord have mercy." The preacher shuffled back two paces. "But now I see."

"Glory Halleluyah," they shouted.

In his early thirties, the preacher was a broad-shouldered and handsome man who moved with uncommon agility for his size. He wore a royal blue suit with a deep burgundy tie and white shirt, the jacket falling well below the length of his arms. His lips were thick and flexible, giving plenty of room for the loose, rich smile, and his face, though fleshy, was pleasant and easy to look into. The preacher had one gold eyetooth, and, when he reared his head back to look toward the sky to address the Lord, it looked like the fang of a black lion growling toward glory. In his right hand he held a folded handkerchief, and when he wiped his brow, the shiny gold ring on his little finger danced over his forehead as he started his sermon.

"Sometimes I looks over my congregation and I asks God, Why, Precious Lord, do my peoples suffer so much? Why is it,

Lord, that some folks got the whole world in they hands and my peoples work so hard, work so hard, Lord, just to get by, just to put bread on they table?

"I was down on my knees just last Thursday morning, brothers and sisters, and I asks the Lord, I says Lord, is my peoples true believers?

"And you know what the Lord say?"

"What'd the Lord say, preacher?"

"The Lord say, listen to me now, peoples. The Lord say, this here right what He said now, 'I know they believes in Me, but do they believes in they selves?' Now that make me jump back when the Lord say that. So I come up off my knees and look straight up in the sky, high as I can, and I come right back to the Lord and I say, Lord, Precious Almighty Lord, what do you mean believes in they selves?"

The preacher wiped his brow and took a deep breath, flaring his nostrils. He stood poised and humble, perhaps to accentuate his privilege of being able to summon God instead of having to wait for Him. "That's when the Lord come on out with it, peoples. Listen to me now, hear what the Lord say: 'Ask,' He say, 'and ye shall receive.' And I said to myself 'Whoa, Lord. Sweet Jesus.'"

The preacher took his Bible and held it high in the air as if to allow the Lord to anoint again its very pages. "Then the Lord told me to go to this here Bible, and I set myself down and read the very first verse my eyes come unto: Matthew 7, verse 7 and 8. Peoples, this here is what the Lord got to say about it: 'Ask and it shall be given you; seek and ye shall find; knock, and it shall be opened unto you; For everyone that asketh receiveth; he that seeketh findeth; and to him that knocketh it shall be opened.'"

The preacher moved from behind the pulpit to as far in front of the platform as he could, tilted his head back, and roared boldly toward the rafters. "They believes in me the Lord said. But do they believes in they selves? Think with me now, peoples. What the Lord saying? What the Lord saying? This here's what the Lord saying: if you believes in Me, peoples, and I'm the one what made all y'all." The preacher waved his hand across the congregation. "Then what's to keep y'all from believing in y'all selves. 'Ask,' the Lord say, 'and ye shall receive.' When you peoples out there see a nice shiny automobile riding down the road, y'all thinking, 'Ooooweeee. I sure would likes to have me a car like that, but I couldn't never ask to have nothing like that 'cause them things is for white folks.' Oh, yeah. I know you peoples. When you stacking up your bossman's firewood on his porch and you see the Missus in there sewing on a brand new sewing machine you be thinking, 'Ooooweeee, Lord, I sure would like to gets my woman something like that, but I knows better than to think we're supposed to have something so fine as that.'

"Listen to what the Lord's saying to you peoples. Ask and ye shall receive and believe in your self. Ask the Good Lord for the strength to get what you want in this world. He'll give it to you. Y'all think a dollar bill know what color hand holding it? Y'all think a sewing machine know what color feets is pumping it?"

The organist started playing a soft hymn and the preacher adjusted his cadence to accommodate it, working now in a raspy, yet inviting whisper toward the congregation, leaning forward as if to soothe them onto the pulpit with him. "The Lord say, 'Ask and ye shall receive,' but he gots to have somebody there to take hold to it. Look around you, brothers and sisters. White folks ain't afraid to do no asking, and they doing a heap of receiving. You got to reach your hand out to get something." The preacher looked toward the sky and stretched his opened palm up as high as he could. "Just reach out and ask the Lord."

"Praise the Lord," they shouted.

"Amen," the preacher said.

The choir sang "Just As I Am," and the preacher walked down in the front and smiled out over the crowd. He fixed his stare on Jefferson, who dared not lift his eyes off his hymnal until the invitation was over.

CHAPTER 7

After church, Jefferson saddled Emma and rode toward Sweetwater Creek to find Newt. He did not yet know whether he would drink the whiskey when he got there. He only knew that he had to get there and see it, touch the bottle to know for sure. He could have chosen the main road and gone up past the store and through the village to the millpond, but he felt like being alone and Emma was easy to work through the woods. Her ears were relaxed, moving like a second-line rhythm to the steady hollow drumming of her feet on the sunken trail. The cool dry air made his head clear, and he began to reflect on the preacher and how he knew it was the Lord's voice talking to him. He wondered if, when the Lord talked to the preacher, He sounded the way the preacher talked or if He sounded the way the Bible sounded when Ida read out of it. He leaned forward in the saddle and sneered in recollection of the preacher's gold tooth glittering toward the heavens as he spoke. Dropping the reins over the saddle horns, he raised his palms toward the sky the way the preacher had done, adjusting his voice to imitate the extolling tone of the sermon. "Here I is, Lord. This here man on this mule they calls Jefferson. I don't reckon I ever had nothing give to me so's I could tell it. Done kept most of my complaints to my own self. But here I is asking to receive, calling for to have like You done said for to do. All I wants me is a good patch of bottom land, Lord, what me and this old mule can run a deep plow through."

Waiting for a sign, Jefferson studied the long strands of sunlight that filtered through the hardwoods and angled to the ground like clear pools of water. Impatient with standing still, Emma shuffled a few steps sideways and blew, so Jefferson picked up the reins and nudged her along a small branch until he hit Sweetwater Creek. He worked her along the creek bank until he spotted Newt standing on a large rock in the shoals, his cane pole pointed at the bobber dancing in the swift current. Newt worked his way back toward the bank, waving to Jefferson as he jumped from rock to rock and grabbed a branch to pull himself up the bank to stand beside Jefferson. The boy put his hand on Emma's forehead and stroked it gently downwards.

"Durn. You got the prettiest mule in Redbone, Jefferson. Look how she holds her head way up high, and them's the longest ears I ever seen on any mule."

"She all right," Jefferson said. "Fetch up that bottle what you done kept for me."

"Me and Addie done got it hid in a hole in the rocks where we keep things we find. Some of it ain't all that good. Turtle shells and things we find in the creek. Addie found an old boot with the sole rotted off in the creek, and he made me put that in there. Just things like that. Addie's up here on the bank somewhere. He likes to get a stick and dig in the ground and find worms and grubs. He won't ever hurt 'em though. He just puts 'em in his hand and watches 'em squirm around. He ate a grub one time, but I could tell he felt awful bad about it. He even cries when I bait a worm on a hook. It's hard to fish with him splashing around in the water, crying about hurting the worms and all. So I just grabbed a few grubs when he wasn't looking and come on down here to try to catch a big old yellow cat. Come on. We'll go get Addie, and I'll take you to where we got that bottle hid at."

Jefferson swung down from the saddle and led the mule by the reins, walking side by side with the boy. Newt stopped, cupped his hands, and sang out, "Addie! Addie Boy! Where you at? Addie? Addie Boy!"

They moved along the trail until it suddenly appeared before them, Jefferson and Newt and Emma stopping all movement as if a big buck deer had stopped in the path ahead. But it was not a buck; it was a body and a boot and the junk sorted in piles and the bottle lying on its side half empty with the cap off and the boy motionless with his shirt up over his white stomach and his back on the ground. The arms lay lifeless at his side, palms up, and the legs were crossed at the ankles. His face was caked and muddy, with the head turned so that the lips were open against the ground.

"Oh Lord," Newt said, falling to his knees. "Something's done killed Addie. He ain't moving."

"See has he got any air moving out his mouth," Jefferson said.

Newt crawled over the top of the body and put his ear down where the boy's mouth met the damp ground and listened. Then he put his thumb under Addie's nostril and held it tightly. He jumped back up quickly. "He does! It's coming out. I can feel it." He clasped his hands together and looked toward the sky. "Thank you, Lord. I can feel air coming out of him, Jefferson. He ain't dead. He just looked it."

"He done got his self drunk is all." Jefferson walked over to the bottle and picked it up, brushing the dirt off the cap before screwing it back on. "Look like this whiskey would of been too strong for him to drink much of."

"Naw," Newt said. "Ain't nothing too strong for him. He'll put anything in his mouth. I done seen him chew on a handful of chicken droppings one time, and he didn't even make a face or nothing."

Newt bent down over the boy and shook his shoulder, making the limp body roll from side to side on the ground. The first sign of life was the black-lipsticked grin as he spit his tongue dirt-free. Newt shook the body again, and Addie's eyes rolled around in his head as if they were attached to Newt's shake rather than to their own sockets. Newt tried to raise Addie off the ground, but his brother's arms slid through Newt's grasp, and he fell back to the ground. Newt stood astraddle of the boy, who was making rapid hissing sounds, punctuated and driven by short blasts of air.

Jefferson tied the mule to a pine sapling and walked over beside Newt, still standing over his brother, who was limp on the ground, eyes crossed trying to gather the sky above him into focus, pawing at the light above him.

"He look like a old drunk catfish, the way he gilling, belly up and all," Jefferson observed.

"Reckon we ought to haul him down to the creek and wash him off?" Newt asked.

"Naw. What if he was to go to thrashing around then break a loose and drown his self?" Jefferson said.

"How much of it you reckon he drank?" the boy asked.

Jefferson picked up the dark bottle and surveyed it against the sun. "'Pends on how much got to his mouth and how much leached to the ground."

"Ain't no way we can take him home like this. I reckon we could say he got a stomachache or something from eating all them grubs, but I'd be afraid she'd end up smelling the whiskey on him. Mama ain't been herself lately. She's been sleeping a lot, even when it's still daylight, but if she ain't in the bed when we get there, ain't no way she could miss all this."

Jefferson bent down beside Addie with his chin in his hand, rolling the sassafras twig from one corner of his mouth to the other. "I reckon we could take him to Ida, see could she tend to him."

"You reckon she'd do it?" The boy turned to face Jefferson, eyes wide. "How we gone get him there?"

"Strap him on Emma, lead him to the house," Jefferson answered.

"I'll see to it you get another bottle. Don't you worry none 'bout that," Newt promised.

Newt grabbed Addie's arms and Jefferson took the feet, and they dragged him over the mule's rear end and adjusted his weight so that his stomach was in the center of the saddle, the arms and legs balanced to hang free. Jefferson took some rope out of his saddlebags, and they tied the boy's feet to one stirrup and his wrists to the other.

Newt took off his shirt. "Let me tie this around his neck to keep his face from getting all scratched up. You go on and lead Emma, and I'll stay back here and walk beside him, make sure he don't slip off or something."

Newt walked beside the mule with his hand ready to catch the suspended, rolling head that bobbed out of the four-beat rhythm of the mule's steady gait.

"Hold up. Hold up," the boy shouted to Jefferson. "He's starting to throw up."

It came at first like the gurgling of water rising to a hand pump, unhinging Addie's mouth and gushing in one loud cascade. The boy opened his eyes, coughed, and then lowed like a cow. He now seemed to give in to the action of his heaving chest, no longer fighting the deep bellows that exploded from the stomach. Jefferson dropped the reins and did not even turn around; he stood with his arms folded, looking down the trail. Newt watched the boy as the heaves became dry and the body finally relaxed, the head free to swing again.

"I believe he's done got it all out," Newt said. He wiped Addie's chin and nose clean with the shirt he had tied around the boy's neck. "I'll clean up this saddle when we get to your house.

Don't worry none 'bout that. I'll wipe it down just as good as new when we get there."

Addie was beginning to awake again when they came out of the woods into the open fields and saw Jefferson's house. He began with a deep moan, then raised his head off the saddle to bawl like a roped calf. Newt stooped down and walked beside him, half whispering, half singing a song that Jefferson did not recognize.

"Oh Lord. He's starting to come around, Jefferson. Looks like he's fixing to bust on out to a fit any minute now," Newt said.

"We 'most there now." Jefferson lengthened his pace as he came to the clearing.

Ida came out of the house as they were untying the boy, moving his body across the mule and lowering him to the ground. She bent down and put her hand on the boy's face, asking no questions, saying nothing. Her resolute expression allayed the uncertainty around her and even the smell of the boy himself. It was as if what she was about to do had nothing to do with what happened, but only with what could be done now, what work had to be done by her hands. They followed her through the front door carrying the boy through the kitchen and into the bedroom. Ida pointed to her room. "Lay him down in my bed."

She returned with a damp towel and cleaned the boy's face, then washed out the rag in the water bowl beside the bed and turned to Newt, handing him the rag. "Take his clothes off him and put the covers over him and keep this here damp rag on his head till I gets back." Newt laid the boy's clothes in a pile at the foot of the bed. Ida worked at the stove while Jefferson sat at the kitchen table, looking into the bedroom at the boy lying in his bed. Newt folded the damp rag and placed it on Addie's forehead, then sat still on the bed beside him, looking around the room.

Ida returned with a bowl of water and a rag. "Y'all get on outside and let me and the boy be."

Addie's eyes wandered across the planked ceiling and walls until his eyes settled on the stream of light angling through the curtain and into the room, the same light that he would wait for on summer mornings when he would rise before dawn and enter the barn to sit within the soft clucking of hens and rustling of the one cow on straw. There, he would wait for the morning to move upon him until he saw it, the first light that would seep between the boards, pale shadows later whitening and flowing with the dust rising off the cool dirt floor. Perhaps he did not comprehend that it was light at all, but he knew something of its warmth. For when the light reached the center rafter of the barn, he would stand up by it to feel of its warmth and then squint into it, one eye at the time, as if studying from where it came until his eyes burned.

Now he felt Ida's forearm brush his thigh near his hip as she smoothed the quilt around his body. She bent over him, taking the stream of light as she came, then touched the cool rag to his forehead, moving it gently down his face to wipe the corners of his mouth. A soft moan rose from within him as her warm hand touched the back of his neck and moved the pillow beneath it. The soft humming of Ida's voice seemed to relax him, and he finally gave his whole body to it.

Newt and Jefferson walked outside and sat on the front steps in the early afternoon sun.

"You reckon that's a sin for him to get drunk like that, with him not even knowing what it was and all?" Newt asked. "I can't say for sure whether he's ever done any real sinning before and all of a sudden here comes one popping up from nowhere and it's all because of me. All 'cause I wanted to catch a dadgum catfish."

Jefferson did not answer.

"I hope Mama don't see nothing wrong when we get home. She's always studying Addie's eyes, and if she sees something that don't look right, ain't no telling what she's liable to do. That Miss Ida sure is good at taking care of folks, ain't she? Lord have mercy. I hope Addie don't give her no trouble. Mama says Miss Ida can even mend a broken bird's wing and get it to eat out of her hand."

Jefferson looked up across the garden and deep into the sky before he spoke. "You gots any money?" he finally asked.

"Not on me. But I got three dollars and a half counting that dollar Papa give me yesterday hid at the house," the boy answered.

"That's it?" Jefferson turned to face the boy with a calculating and intense stare, one that the boy had never seen on him before.

Newt looked down in his lap, scratching the dirt out of his palm with his thumbnail before answering. "I got a gold-plated pocket watch my granddaddy left me. He worked on the Carolina, Clinchfield, and Ohio Railroad for twenty-five years. That was my mama's daddy. They say he was one smart man. It keeps good time, too."

"Bring it all with you when we meet up with Beaucat this Friday," Jefferson said.

"The watch, too?" the boy asked.

Jefferson nodded, then rose up off the steps and walked across the yard to a big pecan tree. He sat down at its trunk, wiggled his back against it until he found a comfortable position, and then angled the felt hat down low over his eyes. The boy followed him over and lay down on the other side of the tree, cradling himself in the roots coming out of the hard bare ground.

Newt awoke when he heard the screen door open. He stood as Ida motioned for him to come in the house. Addie was sitting up in the bed when Newt walked in. He looked better than Newt had hoped. Although his cheeks were hollow and pallid, the eyes had somehow maintained their innocence, even regaining a slight twinkle out of the swollen lids as he recognized Newt; his face was clean, the hair brushed back neatly.

"Doggone, Miss Ida, look like you done rose him from the dead again."

"He be all right once you get him to his own bed," she said, smiling so brightly at Addie that it made him turn his forehead into Newt's shoulder. Newt took the boy's hand and they walked out of the house into the cool shade.

Jefferson, still resting at the base of the tree, lifted his hat and squinted at Newt and the boy.

"Don't worry about getting up," Newt said. "I'll just walk him on home and see if that don't finish getting the wobble out of his legs."

CHAPTER 8

On Friday morning Jefferson steered the truck through the deep clay ruts and down the winding dirt road toward Earl Ham's place. The night before, he had asked Ida to do some figuring for him with a pencil on a paper sack, telling her the numbers she was multiplying and carrying were for a cotton crop he planned to get in that spring. As she multiplied thirty-two times one hundred fifty then multiplied that number times twelve, he did not even dare to speculate what the number would be, afraid that the true and irretractable knowledge of it would threaten the advantage it brought. She bent over the paper next to the oil lamp and slowly measured the numbers out. He wondered if the number would be more or less than the sum of all the bottles he had drunk. But he dared not think too hard on that number either, recalling the numb and restless energy of the whiskey itself and how it would drain down his arms into his fingers like the slow drip of blood from a hog hung to be dressed and quartered.

"Five hundred seventy-six." Her whisper settled through the room. The number was so large that it did not frighten him as he thought it would. Rather, his mind raced ahead to imagine how much good bottomland half of that number would buy. He divined that perhaps this would be the day he would be heard, the prayer that was not so much a prayer as it was the pure and simple recognition that there was an account at all, the balancing of which would be the natural order of its very existence.

When Jefferson rounded the last curve before the Ham place, he saw Newt squatting on a fallen oak limb on the side of the road, holding the burlap bag in his hand. The boy rushed to the truck and hopped in. "I left out early when Mama was reading him a story so we wouldn't have to watch him run after us again," Newt said. "She didn't say the first thing about us coming in late on Sunday evening. When we walked in the kitchen door, she was right there at the stove cooking, and I told her Addie was slap wore out from digging around for worms all day and she looked up and says, 'Y'all didn't get very dirty,' and I said, 'No'm.' And she went back to humming another church hymn over them pots and never even looked hard at us."

Rather than asking Newt the question, Jefferson half-turned and stared down at the boy's waist, eyeing his pockets. Newt obliged, digging out the watch and holding it up by the chain toward the windshield where Jefferson could see it as he drove.

"Mama said this thing's got twenty-something jewels in it, and this chain is fourteen-karat gold. Mama said her daddy held this same watch in his hand every day for twenty-five years when he worked on the Carolina, Clinchfield, and Ohio Railroad. He was from South Carolina. That's where Mama grew up. Sometimes I just hold this watch in my hand and think about his big old hand holding it all them times and it makes me think about him, too. Granddaddy started coming to see us when I was about four. Mama said he never came before that because something had come between 'em. But from everything I could tell, he sure did love my mama. You could see it in his eyes, the way he just looked at her when she walked into a room where he was setting. He'd put whatever he was reading down in his lap and just look at her and smile, not a smile where you could see all his teeth or anything, but just like his whole face was lit up without him even having to try. He sure was nice to me and Addie, too. He wasn't ashamed of Addie none at all. He'd hold his hand and walk right inside Mr. Bludie's store with him. I can't say he cared too much for Papa though. Papa always seemed to be gone when Granddaddy come around. He died when I was nine years old."

Jefferson cocked his head at the boy, a shade of disbelief in his eyes that the boy had stopped talking so soon. "What it was killed him?"

Newt studied the question before he spoke. "I don't reckon they ever really told me what it was. He just died in one day, all of a sudden. Old age, I remember some of 'em saying. Mama told me that one morning after breakfast he said to the lady that cooked for him that he was going back to lay down and take a nap, that he was tired. That was the last thing he ever said, that he was tired. He never did get up again."

They turned off the dirt road and headed down a narrow trail, crossing through a ford in the creek before working their way back up on the ridge.

Newt looked down into the hollows, then turned and addressed Jefferson directly. "I done thought about it all week, you asking me to bring this watch and all my money. Then I thought about you already knowing that Beaucat fella. It all just seemed to add up. You're figuring on us buying a case of that whiskey off Beaucat for ourselves to sell, ain't you?" Newt glanced over to Jefferson, who kept his eyes hard on the road ahead. "I knew it," the boy said, digging a small folded paper from his pocket. "I got a pencil and piece of paper out last night and worked the numbers all the way through. We'll make fifteen dollars and fifty cent profit if we can buy one case from Beaucat on our own and sell it." He paused and looked out to the woods. Finally, he asked, "How you thinking we ought to split that up?"

"I ain't studied it," Jefferson answered, as if irritated at having to address the future at all. Then he relaxed in his seat and focused on the road. "Half, I speck. If you has to put in that old watch."

Newt tilted his hat back and placed his arm on top of the seat where his hand rested near Jefferson's shoulder. "You're the first partner I ever had at anything."

Jefferson moved the sassafras twig over to the right side of his mouth as he pushed in the clutch and changed gears, answering the boy with a muffled grunt through his closed mouth.

They could see Beaucat's place as they came out of the tight canopy of copper-leaved hickories and into the clearing. The large frame house had been a respectable country home at one time, and although the weather had brushed the whitewash clean to the boards and the narrow front porch sagged toward the creek side, the house still looked solid and deep-rooted, as if it could lean into the strongest wind and remain standing. Buggy wheels, rusted plow parts, and old barrels were scattered across the yard, and in the small clearing next to the barn, rock piles sprouting briars and elms meandered through a field that had not been plowed in years. They parked between two black walnut trees that framed the steps of the house and waited in the truck for someone to come out. Beaucat appeared, not from around the back of the house as they had expected, but rising up out of the brushy path coming from the creek bottom. They got out of the truck, walked a few steps toward him, and stopped.

Beaucat looked to be a man in his early fifties. He had a full white beard and was spindly to the point of being elegant. He moved with a casual gracefulness, and, although his pace carried intent, he did not appear to be in a hurry. Beaucat had not gone after the job of being head whiskey-maker in Redbone; he had inherited it, the way a man inherits land or his complexion. He was that delicate paradox of a man who was the best at what he did because be did not seem to care in the least about being the best at what he was doing. Whereas Jefferson wore his hat down low over his eyes as if to hide his face, Beaucat wore his hat simply as an ornament to adorn his head. Beaucat would plop the hat on top of his head to settle on its own accord and angle, and it bestowed a woodsy elegance.

He saw them and smiled with a smile as broad as his beard and several shades whiter, cocking his head slightly to the side as he spoke. "Lord, Lord, Lord. Just look what we got us here. Just look at you, child. Just look at you. Got that light hair and green eyes just like your mama do."

"That's what most folks say, Mr. Beaucat," the boy said, taking his hat off and pushing his blond hair down onto his forehead.

"Mr. Earl, he done told me y'all was coming. Old Beaucat's done got y'all ready to ride."

Beaucat walked over to the woodpile and tossed the top layer of firewood to the side. When he came down to the burlap bags, he yanked them off the boxes the way a woman snatches a dirty sheet off a bed. "Them's y'alls'," he said, pointing. "You can load 'em on up. I gots to get on back down to the creek. She bound to be rattling on good about now and I reckon I best get to stirring 'fore she gets to sticking."

Newt and Jefferson watched as Beaucat's long and easy pace carried him back where the trail began. Newt looked at Jefferson for a clue to their next move, then cupped his hands and shouted, "Mr. Beaucat! We forgot something."

Beaucat turned and looked back up the hill, watching Newt as he walked down to meet him with Jefferson following. Newt stopped in front of Beaucat, pulling off his hat again, working the rim round and round in his hand. "Me and Jefferson got some business of our own we need to talk over with you."

"You is?" said Beaucat, still smiling, but with a hint of gravity in his eyes now.

"Yes sir," the boy started. "We, that is me and Jefferson, would like to buy a case of that moonshine whiskey off of you."

"Lord, Lord, boy. What you need a case of that moonshine whiskey for? You ain't thinking on drinking it, is you? That much whiskey'd wash you down this branch and out into that river," he said, laughing and waving his hand out toward the hills in the direction of the river.

"Naw sir. We ain't aiming to drink it. We know some folks up the road that thinks this is the finest corn whiskey in the whole state of Georgia, and we thought we might help 'em out some since we'll already be going that way and all."

"Uh-huh," Beaucat said, rubbing his whiskered chin and looking at Jefferson and then back at the boy. "Well I don't reckon there'd be no harm in letting y'all buy a case if y'all got a mind to. They's eight dollars."

The boy reached in his pocket and took the money in his hand and looked back up at Beaucat. "We got three dollars and fifty cent cash money on us, and if you was to give us till tomorrow at noon, I was thinking we could bring you back five dollars instead of the four dollars and fifty that we'd owe you and you could make an extra fifty cent for trusting us this one time."

"Lord, Lord child. That there won't work none too good. I can't sell nothing that make a man crazy as this do on credit. Naw sir, honey. You gets your money up next time, and I'll sell you the whiskey then." He turned and started back down toward the creek.

Newt looked at Jefferson, whose puzzled eyes were fixed on Beaucat's shoulders as he ambled across the clearing toward the brush, as if he was watching a wild turkey strut out of the range of his shotgun. Newt waited for Jefferson to make the next move, but he made none, so the boy turned toward the creek and hollered out again, "Mr. Beaucat!"

When Beaucat turned around this time, he saw in the boy's hand a watch hanging from the gold chain as the boy walked toward him. Jefferson followed, stopping to stand behind the boy.

"What you gots there, child?" Beaucat asked.

"It's a twenty-something jewel pocket watch with a gold chain," Newt said. "It belonged to my granddaddy. He was a railroad man."

Beaucat took the watch from the boy's hand, put it up to his ear, and then held it up higher than his eyes to turn it into the sunlight. "What you needs for this old watch and chain, child?"

"I ain't aiming to sell it, Mr. Beaucat. I thought you could hold it for the money we owe you. The way I got it figured, if you was to give us a case of whiskey and take this three dollar and fifty cents, then we'd owe you four dollar and fifty. You could keep that watch till we brought you back the four fifty."

Beaucat looked at the watch again. "I'll give you six dollar for the watch, then you can have the case of whiskey and a dollar and a half boot."

"No sir." The boy stopped moving and stood perfectly still as he spoke. "I can't sell that watch outright, it being my granddaddy's and all."

"Well, I do this here then," Beaucat offered. "I'll keep this here watch, and if you bring me back six dollar 'fore a week from today, I gives you the watch back. If you don't, I keeps the watch."

The boy looked at Jefferson, who could only muster the scratching of his head in a feeble manner. Newt stepped toward Beaucat and stuck out his hand. "We got us a deal, Mr. Beaucat."

They followed Beaucat back up to the house, where he dug out another case from the other side of the woodpile. Jefferson loaded it onto the floorboard of the truck with the rest. Newt moved back in front of Beaucat and spoke in a low voice. "You thinking Papa needs to know anything about this last case?"

"You ain't got to worry your pretty little white head none 'bout that. Your business and my business is my business and your business, child, and Mr. Earl's business and my business is his'n and mine. I just makes it and sells it. Old Beaucat leaves it to the rest of the folks to drink it and fight over it."

Beaucat pulled the watch back out of his pocket and turned it against the sunlight again as if amused to be checking the time of day.

CHAPTER 9

Jefferson steered the loaded truck down the narrow trails of Beaucat's place and back onto the river road. The high thin clouds rushing toward them from the north made him feel they were hustling toward Berner with newfound pace.

Newt rolled down his window and pressed his hand against the wind. "It's kind of hard to believe, ain't it?" he asked. "Us being in business for our own selves and all. It ain't been that long ago I used to wonder how in the world people went about making money and then, plum out of the blue, here we are riding down the road on a Friday morning, in business for ourselves.

"Only thing that keeps it from being near about perfect is me worrying about that watch. I'd sure be feeling good now if I didn't have that to worry about. I suppose if it came down to it, we could sell our case first, then if we couldn't sell all of Papa's whiskey we could take what was left over back to him and tell him we just couldn't sell it all this go-round. He'd cuss us something awful, and Lord only knows what else, but once that was over, we'd still have Granddaddy's watch, so I reckon it'd be worth it."

Jefferson spoke slowly, measuring every word. "I'll sell that saddle if I have to."

"You mean that World War I cavalry saddle? Durn, Jefferson. You'd do that for me? That was your papa's saddle. That's even closer than a granddaddy. Naw. That's mighty nice of you and all. But I couldn't let you do that. I'd feel just as bad about you losing that saddle as I would about me losing that watch. I guess I ought to just quit fretting so much about that watch and worry about making sure we sell everything we got and get back with Beaucat's money. If we do all that right, then worrying about that watch'll take care of itself, won't it?"

"Ain't gone be no need to, though," Jefferson said.

"Need to what?" the boy asked.

"Sell that saddle," Jefferson said, more confident now, digging the sassafras twig behind his eyetooth. "'Cause I ain't gone let nothing happen."

"I know one thing," the boy started again. "We got to figure out some way to sell all that whiskey before it gets real late and get on back to Redbone with the money. If we end up staying all night like we done last time, something's bound to happen. Once all them folks get good and drunk, ain't no telling what all could go wrong."

When they reached Tarentine's Ferry, the wagons were stacked deeper than the last time they had passed. The line wound back up the river, and some of the people had built a fire at the riverbank and were standing around talking, waiting for their turn to load on the ferry. Some of the wagons were stacked with cotton bales coming late out of the fields. Others were piled high with dried ears of corn, ready to take across the river to Bowdoin's Grist Mill to grind into meal, grits, and feed. One wagon carried a black family with six children hanging on the side rails. Their furniture was strapped down with bailing wire, the husked and feathered mattresses on top. The pots and pans hung off the outside of the wagon, and on the front seat an old black woman sobbed without sound into a stained dishrag. Her husband stared across the river with the reins in his hands.

"Pull in there," the boy said. "Look at all these folks that's gathered up around here."

"Naw. We best get on to Berner."

"Come on," the boy urged again. "Let's just pull in there a minute and see what's going on."

Jefferson pulled down the ferry road and parked at the edge of the trees. They walked over to the fire where everybody was listening to a wiry white man talk about a mule he had for sale. They knew who he was. His name was Hap Turnipseed. He stood a few inches over five feet, about the same height as the boy. Hap wore a large loose-fitting straw hat with a narrow pointed brim and a hawk tail feather coming out of the back that made his head appear wider than his shoulders when he turned sideways. Newt leaned against the tree and watched the mule trader work. Hap's features were sharp, the nose lightly beaked over the quick thin lips, the pointed chin falling toward the hickory-nut Adam's apple. His large brown eyes entranced the listener with calf-like innocence while his shins and elbows, which looked as hard as railroad iron, spun the prey into a web. It was the voice, however, that Newt studied the most. Hap's voice had a range that could move from soothing baritone to urgent alto, and he sometimes performed the whole scale in one short phrasing.

His first words about the mule were low and earnest, just above a whisper. "She's a easy keep, too, fellas. Any young 'un can saddle up that mule and ride her." Then he ran the length of the scale, from low to high, as he turned to Newt and pointed. "That boy right there could ride that mule. And plow? Sweet Lordy Jesus, friends. That mule look like she knows where them rows is supposed to go." He bent forward with his hands clasped behind his back and brought his voice down again to a sanctuary low. "I got her off a man what said he had to sell her 'cause his wife died, God rest her soul, and he had to get the casket money for the burying. I wouldn't be a selling her now if my boy hadn't run off. I can't plow but one mule at a time, you see." He tilted his head back and reached the high notes again. "And lope? Good godalmighty, mister gentlemens. That mule can lope just as slow. I tell you fellas what you can do. You can put that mule in a slow lope and ride her all the way to Hillsboro, and when you get off you'll feel like you done rode cross country in a rocking chair."

"What color is she?" a farmer asked.

Hap yanked a smile out of the right side of his jaw and locked his soft brown eyes on the man that asked. "Dapple gray."

"How tall is she?"

"Neighbor, that mule's a plenty tall enough to plow all day and just low enough to hop on and ride." Hap stopped talking and put his hand on his heart as if suddenly struck with an unexpected reverence for what he was about to say. "Give me just a minute, friends. Y'all gone have to forgive old Hap. It's done come again." Hap shook his head as if trying to clear his mind. "The more I get to talking about that mule the more I get took with her my own self. This here soft spot I got"—he stopped to shake a finger gently toward the heavens—"is bound to be the ruin of me. The more I think about it, Sweet Lordy Jesus, help me now, I believe I'll just have to sell that other mule I got and keep that dapple gray."

A black sharecropper stood in front of the man who had been asking the questions. "How much you want for her?"

"Which 'un?" Hap asked.

"That gray mule."

"Well, neighbor. Now that we got somebody else a interfering," he said, pointing to the sky again, "we'll just have to see if we can't square it up between the three of us. If I was to sell her at all, I'd have to get twenty-five dollar for her."

"I'd likes to see that mule," the black man said.

"We'll, ain't no harm in looking, I don't reckon, but I ain't promising nothing, friend. I'm liable to get back up there and just can't bring myself to let that mule go at no price." The two of them walked off with the Hap still talking, his hand resting on the black man's shoulder. Newt listened until Hap's voice faded out of hearing.

The boy, inspired by the way Hap had just worked the crowd, eased through the people and stepped up to the fire with his thumbs locked in his overall loops. "We got a couple bottles of good whiskey in that truck if y'all's interested."

"Ain't no good whiskey 'round here, boy. It's all that muddy water stump."

"No sir. This ain't from 'round here."

"Ain't Sweetwater Creek stump, is it?"

"Yes sir, that's sure what it is."

"Let me taste of it. I'll tell you right quick is it is or is it ain't."

"Come on, then," the boy said, already walking.

They went to the truck and Jefferson took a bottle out, unscrewed the cap, and handed it to the man. He tilted it up carefully to his mouth in both hands as if he was just going to ease a little into his mouth, but when he got it there he turned the bottle up hard and took a long drink.

"Whoa now, whoa," Jefferson said, reaching out to take the bottle from the man's now relaxed arms, "you ain't got to drank it all to see what it is."

"Oooowweeee. That ain't no muddy water stump, y'all," the man finally blew. "That boy telling the truth. How much you asking?"

Jefferson looked at Newt. "Two dollar and seventy-five cent," the boy said.

"Shit, I got to have me one."

They huddled around the man with the bottle and tasted his, then crowded back around the open truck door with Jefferson pulling out the bottles and giving them to the men as they counted out their money to Newt.

"Where'd that stump come from, boy?"

"A friend of ours makes it down the road. His wife's in the hospital in Atlanta, and he's trying to get up enough money to get her well again. We just trying to help him out some."

"What's ailing her?"

The boy turned to Jefferson and said, "It's one of them long, hard to say kinds of sick, but the doctors said she'd do all right long as he could get 'em up enough money to keep her in that hospital where they could tend to her."

There was a crowd of ten or twelve around the truck now, and they started another fire on a piece of bare ground under two sycamore trees. As the ferry dropped off wagons from the other side, the crowd grew larger, more rowdy.

Jefferson drew nearer to Newt and dropped his voice. "They's a white man standing at the edge of them trees been eyeballing us." Newt turned around and looked at the man, and when he did the man emerged out of the tree shadows, walking toward Newt and Jefferson. His walk was not that of a farmer or timber man. Rather, the gait was more a sophisticated stride, as if he was a man who, on occasion, walked for the pure sake of walking. He was dressed in a khaki shirt and pants with a wide black belt and wore a small, tight-brimmed felt hat slightly cocked back on his head. His hair was a sandy red with a touch of gray around the ears, and he combed it straight back and neat. The deep-set eyes were a dark emerald green, and Newt immediately recognized a shyness about him by the way his eyes wandered off when he spoke.

"My name's McAllister, Ethan McAllister," he said, reaching out his hand to the boy.

Newt took off his hat, put his hand out, and shook. "I'm Newt and this here's Jefferson." Then he put his hat back on and waited.

"Whatever you gentlemen are selling must be of quality." McAllister said.

"Yes sir, they seem to think so," Newt said, nodding toward the crowd by the fire.

"Where are you gentlemen from?" McAllister asked.

"Just down the road a ways," Newt answered, eyeing south down the road behind McAllister.

"I rode over from Hillsboro," McAllister offered. "I just bought a little store up there about a month ago. I came here from South Carolina."

"My mama's from South Carolina, too. The low country. Her name's Naomi. Her folks was Dobbs. But once she married my papa that changed her last name to Ham, Naomi Ham. You know any Dobbs where you come from?"

McAllister looked deeply into the boy's eyes as Newt spoke, letting the slow drawl of the boy work through him like warm steam rising off the morning river. He nodded at the words when the boy finished, not in affirmation of what was said, but in admiration of the boy who had spoken them.

"What all y'all sell over there in that store of yours?" Newt asked.

"Oh, just a little bit of everything. Feed, groceries, tools, boots. Whatever people need, I try to have it for them."

"You look a little like the law except you ain't got no big hat on or no gun showing."

"I do, do I?" McAllister said, forcing a laugh. "I can't say I even know the law in this county. You think I could have a taste of what you gentlemen are selling?"

Newt looked at Jefferson, who seemed out of sorts, moving the sassafras twig quickly from one corner of his mouth to the other.

"I don't reckon it'd hurt anything for you try a taste," Newt said, motioning for Jefferson to get a bottle out.

McAllister took the bottle from Jefferson and put it up to his lips and let it sit there for a minute as if he was smelling and tasting it all at once.

"Well, gentlemen. It's no small wonder this is selling. Quality always finds a buyer. How much are you asking?"

"Three dollars," Newt said.

"Three dollars," McAllister repeated, looking over Newt's head at the tree line. "How many bottles have you got left?"

"Eight," Jefferson said, stepping in front of the boy.

"Would you take twenty dollars for the rest of it? That's two-fifty a bottle."

Newt looked at Jefferson again, then turned to the man. "I reckon we could cut you in on a deal, you being new around here and all."

McAllister counted the twenty dollars into Newt's hand. "I could buy two cases of this whiskey, that is, if it's always this good, every Friday afternoon if you could deliver it over to Hillsboro."

"Where'd you say your store was?" Newt asked.

"It's right in Hillsboro," McAllister said. "Just ask anybody when you get there. McAllister's General Merchandise."

"Two cases at two fifty a bottle?" Newt asked.

"If that's the best you can do on your price," McAllister answered.

Newt looked at Jefferson again, and this time Jefferson spit out the sassafras twig, which he had worked to a frazzle_before he spoke. "We be there Friday, mister. If nothing don't happen."

The man stuck his hand out to Jefferson this time, and Jefferson took it not knowing whether to squeeze hard or soft or even how long, having never shaken a white man's hand before.

"We'll see you Friday, then," McAllister said.

They watched Beaucat work around the still and the fire, pouring the bottles and talking to the black mule tied among green saplings, its tail toward the fire. They crept down the trail to see how close they could get, but Beaucat spoke without even turning his head in their direction. He wedged a piece of firewood under the slow blue coals as his words stopped them in their tracks. "Heap of good mens done got theyselves shot, sneaking up 'round a still."

"We wasn't sneaking, Mr. Beaucat," Newt said. "We just got back early. You sure got a pretty place to work around, down here by this creek and all. Jefferson, he didn't want to come down here. He said you might not want nobody tromping down on you. It was all me. I couldn't quit worrying 'bout that watch."

"Watch?" Beaucat stood up from the fire, eyes hard with the words. "What watch that, boy?"

Newt hesitated as if off balance, caught in the middle of a stride. When he finally firmed his footing and came out with the words, they took on a more urgent tone than even he had expected. "That gold watch of my granddaddy's, the one I left with you this morning for that six dollars."

"Lord, child. That old watch'n chain? I done give that to my brother to take to town. He say he knowed a man what'd tell him if that old thing was worth that six dollar you said it was. You know I just can't be taking this and that not knowing what they worth. Plenty of folks trade me chickens and things and I knows what they's worth. For all I knows, that watch might not be worth nothing but two dollar, then, Lord have mercy, child, I be out four."

Beaucat's words stung through the boy's body. He wished to speak without hesitation, but the heart in his throat, at once throbbing and tight, would not let him. He hawked and spit the iron taste over his shoulder like a man. Then he half-turned to gauge Jefferson's reaction, but Jefferson was studying the black mule. Newt turned back to Beaucat, pulling the hat off his head and combing his blond hair straight toward his forehead again. The breathing smoothed in his nostrils, but his green eyes narrowed down to the sharp black of the pupils. He spoke bravely, without waver. "No sir. That watch's got a fourteen-karat chain and twenty-something jewels. It's worth more than any two dollars you just said. We'll just have to all load up in the truck and go find your brother and the man he's showing it to."

Beaucat stared callously at Newt until he was sure the boy had finished. Then he moved toward the boy, his forearms out slightly to his side with fists clinched, stopping to pose, erect and impenetrable, a few feet in front of him. Then his rigid body collapsed into his broad smile, and he laughed deeply with his head tilted back toward the sky. "Lord almighty, child. I's just raising the hair off your hide." His long black fingers pulled the chain from his pocket, the gold watch swaying on the end. "Look a here. Old Beaucat wouldn't do you no harm, honey child." Beaucat turned toward Jefferson and laughed so deeply and freely that Jefferson began to laugh with him.

Newt could not say anything at first; he just watched the gold chain dangle from Beaucat's fingers. "Good godalmighty, and I liked to have said damn with it, Mr. Beaucat. I done heard folks talk about scaring a body to death, but I didn't know that was the way you done it. I thought for a minute all the blood was gonna rise clean out of my skin and I'd be dry as a bone. I ain't never taking that watch out of my room again." Newt took the six dollars out of his front pocket and gave it to Beaucat in one hand and took the watch and chain with the other. Resting it in his palm, he studied the watch as if he had never seen it before. "Just think, for twenty-five years my granddaddy looked at this watch every day, and here I near 'bout went and lost it in one day."

Beaucat reached down and picked up a hickory stick that was as tall as the boy and as thick as his calf. One end was beaten up and frazzled and the other slick and tapered where his hands had held it so many times. He used the frayed end to stir the brew, keeping it from sticking on the sides or settling to the bottom where it would burn. Six washtubs full of sweet corn sat in the bushes, soaking in water. The sugar sacks leaned against a hickory stump, cross-stacked and covered with cedar boughs. Beaucat turned to the boy as he stirred. "Start your fire 'fore dawn, then it'll be burning right good by daylight, give off more heat than smoke that a way. Don't use no real green wood, smokes too much. Folks liable to see it."

As they gathered around the fire and the still, Beaucat knelt and motioned Newt to his side. "Come here, child. Put your finger 'neath that copper wire and let it drip on it."

Newt walked over to the copper tube and squatted down in front of it. "That thing looks kind of like an upside-down snake hanging out a tree and spitting in the water every now and then, don't it?" He let the snake spit on his finger and brought it to his tongue. "This ain't near as strong as I thought it'd be."

"That's the last of that batch, boy. That there's some mighty fine at the end of a batch," Beaucat said.

Newt put his hat on his knee and relaxed his arms on his thighs. "One thing I'll say is we sure do have plenty to drink about if a fella did have a mind to do him some drinking. We done made good money, got my granddaddy's watch and chain back, and ain't nobody opened up no hawk-bill knife on us and tried to take nothing from us. Yes sir. It'd take a mighty judging kind to up and say something 'bout us taking a drink now. Mama, she says we don't never need to judge nobody noways. She says it hard sometimes, though. Real hard sometimes, she says."

Jefferson kept his head cocked at the copper worm dripping into the vat as if still trying to reconcile what the boy had said about the snake.

"You scared of snakes?" the boy asked.

Jefferson, still squatting, rubbed his hands together in front of the fire and held silent.

"I used to be real scared of 'em," Newt said. "When we was little, me and Addie used to go down to the creek swimming, and I'd get him to go down in the bullrushes first and walk around to see if a snake was down there before I'd go in. I felt bad about it, but I ain't gone lie to you, I was so scared of them snakes that I just couldn't help it. One time a big old fat cottonmouth come out right ahead of Addie, but he never would grab at 'em or nothing. It's like them snakes somehow knew he wouldn't hurt 'em, so I tried not to feel real bad about it. Then one day, it just got to where I had done found out about so many other ways to die I just up and quit worrying 'bout getting snake-bit, and from then on we'd just ease on down in them bullrushes together. Where we gonna sleep tonight, anyway, Jefferson? Ain't nobody looking for us to be home till tomorrow."

"Y'all can stay on up at the house with me," Beaucat said. "Ain't nobody stays there but me. We can cook up some beans, ham too, if y'all's hungry."

"We're hungry all right, Mr. Beaucat. We been so busy selling whiskey we ain't even had breakfast yet."

"Let's go on then," Beaucat said. He walked over to the black mule and untied her. Newt followed behind the mule with Jefferson trailing.

At the house, Beaucat stood over the stove slicing chunks of a salt-cured ham into the pot of beans while Newt sat at the kitchen table and counted out the money, laying it out in three stacks on the table. "That squares it," he declared. He pushed the first pile

"You like sleeping?" Beaucat asked.

"I reckon I like it just fine, but I can't say I ever remember that much about it," Newt answered.

"All right, then," Beaucat said, nodding.

"What about heaven, then? You believe He made it just like Jesus promised or you reckon it would of been too hard for Him to make a place where everybody'd be happy all the time, not having to worry 'bout anything?"

"Naw, it ain't that. Once you get to looking around you real good and see how hard it would of been to make what you living in now, all these here little bugs and animals and plants and things, and all of it seeming to work out just like it suppose to, it don't seem like it would of been no harder to make a heaven than all that. Naw sir. He could of done it, I ain't saying that. I just can't see where there'd be no use in it. Goodness'll wear you out sometimes, boy."

"I ain't gone start worrying none 'bout heaven till I gets me some land," Jefferson said. "Then I knows I'll sleep good."

CHAPTER 11

On Monday morning, Ida leaned the basket of laundry against the stair rail at the back door of the Hams'. She opened the screen door and looked out across the fields before knocking. The cotton had been picked and the field plowed through once, leaving only a few stubborn stalks and the occasional white lint, windblown and scrappy across the rows. The sun had gained strength and begun to simmer the dew off the soil. Ida closed her eyes and took in a deep breath of the moist, plowed land.

When Naomi opened the door, Addie stood behind her, his arms around her thigh. "Lord have mercy, Ida. I didn't know you were standing here. You been here long?"

"No'm. Just walked up."

"Come on in here and set that laundry basket down. Have a seat, and I'll get us some coffee."

Naomi's apron slipped from Addie's grasp as she turned toward the stove, and he moved his still-clinched fist to his forehead, knuckling it downward in soft strokes toward the bridge of his nose. His eyes fixed on Ida's smile, then wandered upward as if following some magical draft of air that rose toward the ceiling. Ida picked him up and sat with him in her arms. She cradled the back of his neck in her hand, rubbing her thumb gently behind his ear.

"How's my big boy this morning?" she asked, turning his head with her hand to make him look into her eyes.

"Bless his heart," Naomi said, turning from the stove. "I keep praying that one day he'll say something I can understand. It'd do my heart good just to hear him say 'mama.' Something's troubling him, Ida. I can't help wondering if Earl hadn't scared him some way, figured some kind of meanness to try and make him brave. When he goes to bed at night, he stares up at the ceiling for hours before he falls to sleep. It's like he's waiting for something to come to him. I don't know what could be worrying this child."

Ida combed the boy's hair off his forehead with her fingers and looked deep into his eyes. "Maybe the Lord comes to touch him every now and then, Miss Naomi, knowing he's so troubled."

Naomi moved with the grace of a smaller woman even though she was tall and broad-shouldered. She sat at the kitchen table and poured the coffee into two porcelain cups, then rested her forearm on the table and relaxed her head downward, the soft, green eyes deep in her apron. Her hair was blond, and the grey at her temples feathered the color to an even lighter shade, like brushed steel. Her nose was fine lined but not sharp or ill natured, and she held her mouth in an agreeable part, hinting at a smile that was once pleasing, effortless.

"It's Newt I'm really worried about, Ida, him being gone on Friday nights. Jefferson must have told you what they're doing, where they're going. All Newt'll say is that he's helping out his papa."

"No'm." Ida did not look up from Addie's eyes. "He ain't say."

Naomi leaned forward, arms resting on her thighs, to summon Ida's eyes into hers. "Something's going on, Ida. I found money hid in Newt's room, and the gold pocket watch that his granddaddy gave him was gone Saturday. It's back in there this morning, but I just can't believe he'd take that watch out of this house. He had over eight dollars hidden in the drawer with that watch. I don't know whether he was keeping that money for Earl, or if he got it on his own. How in God's heaven could a child get that much money on his own?"

Ida rocked back and forth with the boy's head on her shoulder. "Jefferson bought me that quilting thread, and I done started a Bear Claw quilt."

"A Bear Claw," Naomi repeated slowly as if mesmerized by the words.

"Ain't no need to go on worrying, Miss Naomi. I speck Mr. Earl just paying 'em a little something for working."

"Ida, Earl wouldn't pay a boy any eight dollars for work. No ma'am. If there's any money around here, it stays in his pocket."

"Last Sunday, Jefferson went to church with me," Ida said, smiling with her hand in front of her mouth. "Sure did. Sat right down in the pew and listened to me sang."

"Jefferson went to church?"

"Yes'm, he did."

"Has he quit his drinking, Ida?"

"No'm. He doing better though. He gone do right one day. I knows it."

Naomi sipped her coffee and looked out the window. The flash of a crow's wing catching wind as it landed in the field caught her eye. It hopped stiff-legged across three rows and pecked at a black clump, then struggled back up to labor against the steady breeze coming over the hedgerow. She stared into the spot where it had disappeared as if she could see something still farther in the distance. "Sometimes I can't help but wonder if I wouldn't be better off taking Newt and Addie back to South Carolina to live with my brother, leaving Earl and this old wore-out red land behind.

"When we first got married and came down here to Redbone, Earl worked hard to make a good life for us. We would go to church together before Addie was born. Sunday afternoons we would ride the countryside and look at the fields he was sharecropping out or a piece of land that he was hoping to buy.

He traded hard all right, but back then he treated people with a measure of respect. For the first few years, I even thought Earl might turn out to be a good man. But he turned hard, Ida. I guess I just kept hoping for the best because Earl's mother was a good woman, a fine Christian woman. She stayed by Earl's papa when the Depression came and he lost everything he had—all his good low country land, cotton gin—lost it all. But there was no end to the meanness in that man. It followed him right to his grave, too. Earl swore to his daddy that he'd get it all back for him one day, and I don't guess he'll quit until he does."

Ida listened intently, her face relaxed and positioned fully toward Naomi's words as if she were warming her cheeks in the sun. "Money steals some folkses' heart away, don't it, Miss Naomi?" she asked.

"It sure stole Earl's papa's. He never did think Earl would amount to anything. Earl's mama told me that sitting right here at this table. Earl told me one time that he'd give half of what he had for his papa to see what he's built here at Redbone. But that wouldn't have been enough for his papa. There's no such thing as enough for a man who lost everything. Lord, Ida. Would God ever forgive me for breaking up this family? I've prayed about it so much, I know the Lord must be thinking, 'Why don't that woman just quit that same old prayer and go on and do what she knows she's got to do.' I wouldn't blame Him. I guess the truth of it is I'm afraid, afraid of leaving and afraid of staying, seeing Newt turn into a man like Earl."

"No'm," Ida said firmly. "That Newt, he a good boy. He gone turn out."

"His teacher told me he was the smartest one in his class. But Newt says he'd rather be doing than studying. She says he could go to any university he wanted to, if he'd just try. Ida, that boy can add up numbers in his head faster than I can write them down and add them."

"And he do love this baby boy, don't he?" Ida said, looking down in Addie's eyes again.

A glimmer of pride flashed in Naomi's eyes. "Sometimes when I look into Addie's eyes and his eyes reach mine, even for just a second, I can see that all that's pure and good in this world is somewhere close at hand. But I'm so tired, Ida. I don't know if I've got strength enough to find my way to it anymore."

"The Lord'll show you the way, Miss Naomi. He always do."

"I know everybody around here's saying that Earl's got other women. I'm no fool. I been knowing that. I can smell that much on his old clothes. But that's not what bothers me. It's these boys that worries my mind, Ida, what Earl will make out of them if he gets half a chance."

Naomi sat up straight in her chair, smoothing the blouse at her chest with the back of her hand, neck arched gracefully. "I had me a good man one time, Ida. Back home in the low country. His family, they could barely make ends meet. They farmed, but they weren't really cut out for farming. Papa said he was lazy and never would amount to anything. His family was just trying to work a poor piece of land was all. I can see that now. We used to meet down by the Salkehatchie River, and he would read me poems from a book of Shakespeare. They were sonnets, Ida, with words as rich and beautiful as you've ever heard." She touched her breast with a clinched fist. "I can still hear the sound of his voice as he read them. Papa, he talked me out of marrying him. I use to blame Papa, but, Lord, I quit that a long, long time ago. The Depression made folks think different. Earl had a little money, and when you got nothing, it makes having enough seem like the most important thing there is in the world, the only thing. Time you figure out it's a lie, it's too late to do anything but live through it."

"Ain't never too late for something good to happen. You knows that, Miss Naomi."

"Ida. I need you to do something for me. Find out what's going on with Newt."

Ida, having listened to every word, gave a shy but noble glimpse of her uplifted chin. "Yes'm."

Naomi straightened up in her chair, lifting her own chin slightly toward the boy. "The preacher always said you could see God in his eyes."

Ida adjusted the boy's head slightly toward the window to better angle the light into his eyes. "Yes'm," she nodded. "Ain't no trouble seeing it, for them what's got eyes to see."

Naomi sat down at her desk by the front window and watched Ida walk across the plowed field in a deliberate and attentive gate, hands clasped behind her, studying the ground as she went. Ida stooped, gathering the overhang of dress in one fist and a handful of soil in the other. Rolling it in her palm, she let it sift through her fingers as if to test its moisture, its texture. She looked back at the windows of the house and stared for moments as if she had left something behind, then walked through the field without stopping again.

The book of sonnets lay open on Naomi's desk. She dipped her pen to begin where she had left off. She had copied by longhand every sonnet she could remember him reading to her. She no longer knew how many times she had written each one. It made her remember the river and the taste of salt in the breeze, the moistness of his lips, rounding the words as he read. She wrote out the last two lines, a couplet that she had memorized long ago.

"For thy sweet love remembered such wealth brings
That then I scorn to change my life with kings."

CHAPTER 12

Early Friday morning at the sawmill, Earl sat at the desk in his office, waiting for Newt and Jefferson. Picking up the photograph of Governor Talmadge, he moved the cigar into his back teeth the way he had seen the governor do when the train stopped in Redbone for his campaign speech. Talmadge had said something in that speech that had not set well with Earl, how the poor white farmer should rise up to take hold of his own destiny, but Earl had worked hard for the campaign just the same, spreading around enough cheap whiskey to swing the county vote. In return, he had hoped for an appointment to the State Board of Paroles, an appointment he was told would reap great dividends. But when Earl put on his best suit and drove to the capital to meet with the governor, he waited in the lobby all afternoon while men less dressed than he got their audience with Talmadge and left smiling. One of the governor's boys finally came out with an autographed picture inscribed, "To Earl Ham, Couldn't have done it without you, Your Friend, Gene Talmadge." The man put his arm around Earl's shoulder and eased him to the door, explaining that a piece of legislation of great magnitude and importance had come up. The governor knew Earl would understand "'cause everything he did, he did for hard-working folks like Earl."

Ham angled the picture toward the light from the window so he could read it clearly. He spoke in a husky whisper, no louder than the rustling of corn stalks. "Papa never had him no autograph picture of the governor. If that old bastard was alive today, he'd see what I done made out of nothing but a bunch of wore-out land and poor folks."

Earl locked the door to his office, pulled down the window shades, and pivoted the side table out from the wall to open the safe. Across his desk, he sorted out the cash, deeds, mortgages, silver coins, and a pistol. Picking up a silver coin, he rubbed his thumb across its rough edges, recalling the Argentinean, the way his dark eyes glistened when he opened the trunks full of coins. Earl counted out enough money to pay Beaucat for the whiskey, stuffing it in his shirt pocket. Leaning back, he surveyed the spread of wealth on his desk and lifted his nose slightly upward the way a coyote scents a new patch of hunting ground. Earl had always said he loved the smell of money, the musky scent it held of man, the stain of plow lines and gun powder and cotton bolls and even the brief aroma of the coffee cans that held it hidden under the planks of drafty shacks.

The shade rattled when Newt knocked on the door. Earl rustled the papers back into the safe and put the Smith and Wesson in his rear pocket. He walked over to the door and cracked it open. "Godalmighty damn. Look like a black plow mule and a yellow billy goat done got hitched up. Bring y'all's asses on in here and set down. I been waiting on you boys."

Earl took his seat and picked up the picture on his desk, turning it so Newt and Jefferson could see it. "Y'all know who this man is?"

"Governor Talmadge, ain't it, Papa?" Newt answered.

"You bet your sweet ass that's who it is, boy. Governor of the great state of Georgia. If it hadn't been for old Earl, he wouldn't be setting in that governor's seat, getting that fancy-ass picture made neither." Earl clinched his fist and struck his chest twice. "By God, I carried this whole county for that man. And don't think he don't know it either. Just look on that picture there, boy, and read what it says. Read out loud, so Jefferson can hear. Hell, he can't read none."

"To Earl Ham," Newt read, "Couldn't have done it without you. Your Friend, Gene Talmadge."

"What'd I just say? What'd I just tell you, boy? One day you liable to see your old pappy setting in that chair. How'd you like that, boy? Governor Earl Ham. Got a ring to it, don't it? That'd make you the governor's son, boy. You'd get all the poontang you could stand then. Godalmighty damn. I reckon we'd have to keep that brother of yours out of sight long enough to get elected else folks liable to think we got bad blood or something."

Newt sat forward with his elbows on his knees, resigned to bearing the brunt of the words as if leaning into a cold pelt of rain, knowing from experience that the least resistance would weather the storm best.

Earl cleared the looseness from deep within his throat without spitting, then stuck the cigar into his back teeth and leaned forward, the seriousness of what he was about to say etched in his brow and confirmed in the narrowing of his pupils. "I been doing me a heap of studying on our little enterprise goings on, and it all keeps a boiling down to the same damned thing. We ain't living up to our potential. We got us plenty to sell, by God, we just ain't selling plenty." He waved his cigar loosely at them and looked away, irritated at having to state the obvious. "That plain enough for y'all?"

Newt touched the wad of bills in his front pants pocket to make sure they were not bulging. "Folks sure got nice things to say about the whiskey, Papa. It ain't that most of 'em don't want it. They do. But money seems real hard to come by for most of 'em. A lot of 'em have to get two or three folks together just to get one bottle."

"Hard to come by?" Earl growled. "Excuses don't make nothing but a trail to the poor house, boy. Y'all got to make 'em want this whiskey so bad they'd sell the only mule they got to get 'em some. Fuck a bunch of 'hard to come bys.' Don't you know them folks's got money stuffed in every little old crook and cranny in them shacks? All y'all boys got to do is just come through there like a high rolling wind and shake it all loose like pecans off a tree."

Newt cast his eyes delicately on his father in an effort to soften the rough measure of his tone. "Jefferson, he done some mighty pretty work last week, Papa. He put on a real fine preaching just to finish selling what we had. You ought to heard him. He made me think about that little fella from Alabama that come through here last winter, getting folks to buy all them skinny mules he was selling."

Earl leaned back in his chair, spit out a loose strand of tobacco, and then blew a narrow stream of white smoke from his tight lips as if he was whistling it out. He watched the smoke rise until it disappeared into the ceiling, then leaned forward and looked hard at Jefferson, then Newt. "Boys, let me get something straight here so's y'all can understand how it works in the business world. We in the selling business. And all people in the selling business has got what fancy folks is calling quotas. That means y'all got to start selling one more case of moonshine whiskey a week and that don't just mean this week. That means ever week y'all got to sell one more than the last 'un. That's what I'm making y'all's quota."

Earl leaned back in his chair again, the satisfaction of what he had just said growing within him until he appeared overcome with satisfaction, suddenly divined with a revelation. "Great godalmighty damn. I just heard myself what I been saying. Here I am learning you boys enough to get y'allselves a business degree in money making, and I'm paying y'all. Damn if that ain't ass backards. It's a good thing my pappy ain't alive to hear all this. Aw hell, I reckon I was just born with a generous nature. When y'all boys get y'all's little end of this business up to eight cases a week, I'm gone look into a little bonus money, throw y'all an extra dollar or two here or there. How'd you boys like that?"

Out of patience, Earl grumbled something incoherent as he stood and reached in his shirt pocket, then handed the bills to Newt. "Here's the money to take to Beaucat. Y'all take five cases and don't bring back no whiskey. No trading like I said before. Just cash money."

Newt and Jefferson, shouldering the weight of Earl's new business plan, slumped into the truck and headed toward Beaucat's. They rode in ruminative silence as Newt strained to recall every word of his father's instructions. Jefferson had already turned the truck off the river road toward Beaucat's before Newt realized how far they had driven.

"I sure wish he wouldn't of said all that. I did learn one thing from in there. It don't take very long for one person to say enough to complicate things to no end for another one. I'm gonna have to take all this figuring out of my head now and write it down on paper. We got Papa's five, two going to Hillsboro. How many more you think we ought to get? Just for us to sell?"

"That man at the ferry say bring three, and I speck we can go to Isaac's, sell three more."

"Durn, Jefferson. Two to Hillsboro, three to Isaac's, three more at the ferry, and five for papa. That's thirteen."

"How much that be if we sell it all?"

"I ain't got that far ahead yet. I'm still trying to figure on how much money we got so we can see how many cases we can buy from Beaucat. Then I'll be able to start figuring on how much we're gonna make on it all."

Jefferson reached in his overalls and handed Newt his tightly rolled bills, tied with a piece of twine.

"That's seventeen you got plus my eighteen makes thirty-five," Newt said. "We're short twenty-nine if we aim to get eight cases on our own." He recounted the money over and over again. "I thought of something that might work but I'm scared to even say it."

Keeping his eyes hard on the road, Jefferson cocked his head slightly toward the boy and waited, letting the frazzled sassafras twig angle loosely toward him.

"What if we—" Newt began, then stopped and looked out the window, allowing his nerve to gather momentum with the fast-paced tree line swishing by. "What if we borrowed the money Papa gave us to buy his whiskey to buy our whiskey instead? We could tell Beaucat that Papa said that he'd settle up with him tomorrow. Then once we sell all of ours and Papa's, we could bring Papa's money back over here to Beaucat like Papa had sent us back over here with it. Only thing is, I ain't sure I can bring myself to tell Beaucat a flat-out lie."

"I'll tell him," Jefferson offered.

"Naw," Newt decided. "I'd be afraid if you told him, he might get suspicious, seeing as how I been doing all the money-handling."

Newt recounted the money once more, then shuffled it from one pile to the other, exhausting all the mathematical possibilities he could imagine. He took his hat off and set the two piles of money inside of it to narrow the possibilities down to a small space before him. He studied Jefferson for a few moments out of the corner of his eye, then lifted the upside-down hat to his chest and looked inside of it the way a deacon checks an offering plate while walking it to the pulpit. "We could tell Beaucat that Papa said he'd have his money to him no later'n noon Saturday. And since Papa intended for us to give him the money now, that wouldn't be a lie because *now* is before noon Saturday. Then, after we get done selling all the whiskey, we'll have the rest of the money to take back to Beaucat. That way he'd have all the money owed to him before noon Saturday and everybody'd be square."

Jefferson nodded almost imperceptibly and rolled his jaw, still working the cud of what the boy had just said.

"That settles it, then," Newt said, moving the plan ahead. "I'm gonna put enough of Papa's money in with ours to give us enough to buy our eight cases, then wrap it up in that piece of twine. That'll make the money look more like ours than Papa's. Beaucat won't ever think Papa'd keep his money wrapped up in an old piece of twine. Besides, Beaucat buys all his sugar from Papa. He won't be worried about getting that money."

Beaucat was sitting on his front porch, pipe in his teeth, hat tilted high off his forehead, when they pulled into the yard. He walked down the steps to meet them under the walnut tree as they dismounted the truck. Newt had opened the truck door before Jefferson had even shut down the engine. "We need thirteen cases, Mr. Beaucat."

"Lord, Lord, child," Beaucat said, angling his hat sideways to shade one side of his face from the sun. "What's your hurry this morning?"

"Papa's got us on something he calls a quota. We got the same amount of time to sell twice as much, so we're in a hurry."

"Thirteen," Beaucat cogitated slowly, as if recollecting the work, the process that went into making each gallon. "When you asked me how much whiskey I could make, you *was* snipping at my heels, boy, and I never even knowed it."

"I was wondering if you cut that whiskey with any special kind of water or just any old water?" Newt asked.

"That well water yonder," Beaucat said, pointing to the hand pump by the kitchen door.

"You reckon we could borrow some water from you and some extra jugs?"

"Help yourself, boy."

"We'll need thirteen of them jugs, too," Newt said.

"Now them jugs is fifteen cent apiece," Beaucat said. "That's what I has to give for 'em."

They carried the whiskey to the hand pump by the kitchen door, and Newt rinsed out the washtub and filled it full of water. Beaucat relit his pipe and relaxed on the back steps with his long leg resting lengthways over the kneecap of his other one. He stretched his foot up and down in an amused rhythm as he watched Jefferson pour the top part of every bottle out into the empty gallons while Newt dipped a ladle of water from the washtub into the bottles, filling them full again. After they loaded the whiskey in the bed of the truck, they borrowed the black tarp from the hood of Beaucat's old Ford to cover it. On top of the tarp, they piled old tires, part of a truck axle, bricks, and hubcaps.

Newt walked toward Beaucat holding out the money rolled up and tied with twine. "Here's the money for what we're getting. Papa wanted me to make sure and tell you that he'd settle up with you for his five cases no later than noon tomorrow."

Beaucat glanced at the money tied with twine. He scratched his hairline behind his ear, tilting the back of his hat upwards so that the brim settled just above his eyes. He studied Newt over the roll of money that he now held at eye level as if it were a tool to measure some dimension of the boy. "They say that sheriff up in Hillsboro don't take to no Jasper County whiskey coming up in his county."

"We'll be real careful, Mr. Beaucat. But you ain't got to worry none about us. That place couldn't be no worse than some other ones we already been to."

CHAPTER 13

Newt relaxed in the front seat, paying no attention to how Jefferson maneuvered the truck in and out of the ruts leading from Beaucat's toward Hillsboro. The crisp air drafting through the open window began to clear his mind, and he thought about the thirteen extra bottles they now had from cutting each case of the whiskey with one gallon of water, adding thirty-three dollars to their profit. The money was adding up faster than he could decide what he wanted to do with it. He wondered what he could buy his mother that would make her happy. But he knew of no gift that was sure to lift her spirit. He had watched her lean against the kitchen window sill with a broom in her hand, letting her eyes drift across the red-stubbled land and settle into the banks of cool grey clouds that hung in the horizon. That was the first time he had sensed something unfamiliar, unsettling about her. It was as if the sadness that she had nursed for as long as he could remember had finally muscled its way to consumption, hardening her features and making her look older. As he watched her that moment, he feared that he had never really known her at all, that perhaps she had lived lives that were unknown to him and always would be. Yet he could feel the pain kneading in her stomach as if it were his own. He thought back on the time when his uncle Will had come down from Beaufort just after Addie was born and loaded them all up in his car. He still remembered driving through a town at dusk, the clean white shacks in the red sunset, with his mother crying quietly into a lace handkerchief, Addie in her lap. Was that the town of Hillsboro? Could that be where he was now returning?

He shifted in his seat and studied the bed of the truck to see how the junk was riding on top of the whiskey, checking for any signs that the whiskey could be seen. Satisfied, he turned back to look ahead, glancing over at Jefferson's tight-skinned jaw and determined eyes before he spoke.

"You think cutting liquor is wrong, Jefferson, as bad as breaking one of them Ten Commandments? I reckon you could look at it like a blessing in disguise if you wanted to. I mean, folks don't get as drunk on cut whiskey, and that makes 'em less liable to do things that'll get 'em in trouble. But on the other hand, they might have to buy more just to get as drunk as they planned on getting in the first place and spend money they ain't got no business spending. Lord, I don't reckon there's no way to look at it that figures all the bad out of it."

Newt stretched and looked out the front window, surveying the road that lay ahead with a newfound confidence. "I been thinking. You know what we ought to do? When we make enough money, we ought to spend some of it to help out folks that really need it. Every time we'd see something good that needs being done, why, we'd just up and do it. Before long, I bet it'd be just like an old habit we couldn't break even if we tried.

"I was riding with Papa one day over towards Buford Crossing and there were some children over there in the mill village that were so skinny you could see their ribs showing. Their eyes were real hollow looking, too. Some of 'em were off in the road ditch getting white clay out of the bank and putting it in their mouths and eating it, even the little bitty ones. Papa slowed down and looked hard at them children. Then all of a sudden he just stopped the truck and reached in his pocket and threw a coin over toward one of 'em. It was a half dollar I think. The biggest boy picked it up and bit it with his teeth; he almost looked like he was foaming at the mouth or something. I asked papa about it. He said you can't help folks that don't want to help their selves but I sure would like to have tried. If we make any money, I want you to drive me back up there one day and let me take 'em a box of groceries or something. I figure that'd be about as good a place for us to start as any."

Jefferson looked over to the boy as if he had been speaking in tongues. "If you's so set on figuring, how 'bout figuring on how much we gwine make if we's to sell it all. Once we get ours then go to figuring on other folks's."

When they got to the crossroads, the sun hovered white and low above the hedgerows, and the patches of dew glistened in the furrows like moist spider webs. Hillsboro was situated at the southern end of a large ridge that stretched out eight or ten miles from town in a north-to-northeast direction. Its rich clay soils gave rise to easy-rolling hills and pastures, occasionally broken by small pecan or apple orchards. The old-timers in the county had always said that before the Depression, you could ride a wagon all the way out the Hillsboro road in early June and never lose sight of a cornfield.

Most of the families that had settled there were Scotch-Irish and had come from South Carolina in the early 1800s. Although the people around Hillsboro lacked the rough edge and quick wit of the people who lived on the river, they were endowed with that certain air of patience and resolve that owning good land breeds. The town nestled quaintly on the ridge top, and the steeple of the Methodist church rose out of its highest point, giving Hillsboro a pious yet lonely appearance.

"There it is," Newt said. "McAllister's General Merchandise. Ride by it real slow at first so we can look around some before we stop." Two old men sat on a bench on the front porch, their heads slightly bowed and close together. As the truck passed by, their white and bearded faces twisted out from under their brown felt hats to follow it past the store.

"They're liable to think it's mighty funny us riding by slow and then turning around and stopping," Newt said. "We better just pull on around back and I'll go in and find Mr. McAllister. You stay with the truck."

On the store's back porch, Newt turned the knob of the heavy pine door and quietly slipped inside. He eased the door shut behind him and found that he was in a small office that had books on shelves from the ceiling to the floor, many bound in deep burgundy with gold lettering. The door leading into the store was cracked open, and he recognized McAllister's voice speaking with a woman. He peered around the door and saw him boxing up the woman's groceries at the front counter. Quietly working his way against the back wall of the store, Newt stood behind the barrels filled with shovels and hoes until the woman left.

Then he stepped out and walked toward the counter with his felt hat in his hand. "Good morning."

Startled, McAllister turned quickly from the ladder he was climbing to stack can goods on the shelves. "Newt. I didn't hear you come in. I wasn't sure whether you would show up or not. It's good to see you."

"We parked around the back, and I come in that way. I left Jefferson out there with the truck. We got just what you asked for last week."

"Good. Good. How've you been?" McAllister asked.

"About the same, I reckon. Ain't a whole lot changed, except Papa's got us where we got more to do and less time to do it in."

"Well, let's go on out back then and see what we've got."

Outside the back of the store, Jefferson heard the gravel slur of a car pulling up slowly behind him, and he slid down in his seat, not even daring to turn and look at what kind of car it was or who was in it. He kept his eye cut at the passenger's side mirror until the large white hat and black leather gun strap appeared, magnified and out of proportion as it swayed closer. Two white hands rested on the window first, followed by a silver badge on the right pocket leaning down, and then a jutted jaw appeared with a matchstick rolling from one corner of the mouth to the other. The man looked at Jefferson for several seconds, his eyes patient and expressionless, before he said anything. "You ain't lost, is you, boy?"

"Naw sir, naw sir, I's—"

"You ain't from 'round here. Is you, boy?"

"Naw sir, I's from Re-Redbone, sir."

"Redbone," the sheriff repeated. "Redbone. That's a long way from Hillsboro, ain't it?"

"Me and that boy, me and that boy, my boss man's boy, we just—his papa sent us down here. He gots a sawmill d-d-down in Redbone, sir."

"He d-d-do, do he?" the sheriff asked.

"Ya-ya-yaw sir, he sure do. That's Mr. Earl."

"Uh-huh. Mr. Earl, you say?"

"Yaw sir." Jefferson nodded.

"This here Mr. Earl from Redbone got his self some business up here y'all tending to for him?"

Coming out of the store's back door, Newt felt as if he had suddenly appeared in someone else's dream and all motion had stopped with his arrival: the sheriff's car parked behind the truck, the square face leaning in the window, and the whites of Jefferson's eyes as he stared not at the sheriff but out the front of the truck. Newt froze on the porch as McAllister brushed past him.

McAllister called out as he descended the stairs, "Good morning, Sheriff. It's good to see you."

The sheriff put his forefinger and thumb on his hat brim and squeezed it off in one gesture, giving a partial nod.

"What you think about these boys driving all the way from Redbone to try to sell me some lumber?" McAllister asked. "I've been considering adding a little lumber yard right out back here. This young gentleman here is Newt, Sheriff. Be careful, though. He drives a hard bargain."

"Mr. Earl's young 'un," the sheriff said.

"Yes sir." Newt started down the stairs toward them. "Papa's always wanting to sell more of something. This sure is a real pretty town y'all got over here, Sheriff."

"Most folks 'round these parts get their lumber from Tuggle over in Berner," the sheriff said, walking around to the back of the truck. "What y'all got all these old tires and junk in here for?"

"Aw, we just can't seem to pass nothing by that somebody'll let us load up for nothing or we see laying on the side of the road. We're always thinking somebody might give us ten cent for this old tire or that old plow part. Just trying to see if we can't make a little something extra. We got a big old pile of junk at the house we sell out of. I reckon we'll just add this to it. You see anything in there you might want and we'll take it out and clean it off and let you take a good look at it."

"How old are you, son?" the sheriff asked, walking back toward them.

"Thirteen," Newt answered.

"Ain't you supposed to be at the schoolhouse?"

"Well, yes sir, and no sir. I am supposed to be at the schoolhouse being just thirteen and all like you said, but my papa's done made some arrangements with the schoolteacher to get me out some Fridays so I can help him out. So she knows about it and all."

The sheriff bent down and looked at Jefferson again in the truck. "This 'un here looks like he done seen a ghost."

"He just ain't used to leaving Redbone. That's all it is," Newt said.

The sheriff reached into the back of the truck and lifted an old axle up as if to test its weight. It clunked, hollow and muffled, as he let it drop. He turned back toward Newt, taking the match out of his mouth before he spoke. "Y'all be careful now. I wouldn't want nothing bad to happen. Wouldn't want y'all to get lost or nothing in my county." He looked over his shoulder at Jefferson as he walked off. "Y'all being so far away from little old Redbone and all."

"Thanks for stopping by and checking on things, Sheriff," McAllister said.

"Good godalmighty," Newt said after the sheriff drove off. "I thought my heart was gonna jump clean out my throat it was beating so hard. I bet y'all could hear it."

"I don't know the sheriff all that well yet, but everybody around here seems to think he's all right," McAllister said.

"I don't reckon he'd of been all right if he'd of made us take some of that junk out of the back to look at," Newt said. "Reckon what he'd of done if he'd of seen or smelt that whiskey?"

"I don't know," McAllister admitted, shaking his head. "They say the sheriff's been in with Tuggle and his whiskey business around here for years. The problem is, nobody much wants Tuggle's whiskey anymore."

Newt bent down beside the truck window and put his hand on Jefferson's shoulder. With his hands still gripping the steering wheel, Jefferson slowly turned and looked up at Newt, his eyes a porcelain glaze that showed no signs of focus. Newt shook his shoulder. "Get on out, Jefferson, and let's get these boxes to where Mr. McAllister wants 'em." They each carried a case into the office and McAllister unlocked the closet door.

Newt turned in a slow half circle, surveying the office shelves. "I ain't never seen so many books in one place. This here's more'n we got at the whole school. Have you read every one of 'em?"

McAllister reached up and touched one of the books with his fingertips. "I read every chance I get. It's like a little library. Folks around here can come and borrow a book to read if they want to."

"What are most of 'em about?" Newt asked.

"History, literature. Law mostly. I practiced a little law in South Carolina before I came here. The rest of it is just a little bit about everything you can imagine."

"My mama reads all the time, too. She says she named me after a man named Sir Isaac Newton. She said he might have been the smartest man that ever lived, him finding gravity and the way colors work and all."

"She's named you well. He was a brilliant man," McAllister said. "Do you like good stories?"

"I like the ones Mama tells about the old times in South Carolina, when the Depression first came and everybody had to learn to scrape just to get by," Newt answered. "All the things they had to do just to get from one day to the next. You know, about how they had to eat possums and greens and use the same coffee grindings for two or three weeks. Things like that. Granddaddy said you could tell that the worst of the bad times was over when a rabbit took off running down the road in town and didn't nobody get up to chase after it. Mama said the folks who happened to end up with old poor sandy land just couldn't make it when times got real rough. She said it wasn't no fault of theirs really. They worked just as hard as everybody else, but they just couldn't make that land give 'em what they needed."

"A lot of people back where I came from were forced off their farms by the banks because their land wasn't good enough for them to make a living on," McAllister said. "But I guess here in the south we have it better in some ways than they do in the north. When they get hungry and have nothing to eat, they have to stand in a soup line and count on someone else's generosity to feed them. But down here if a man's resourceful enough he can run a trot line or hunt or trap food, even pick a mess of polk salad if he has to."

Newt eyes brightened. "I never thought about it like that. I guess we are mighty lucky."

"I'll tell you what," McAllister offered. "I'll find you a good story out of these books and let you borrow it next time I see you."

"I'd like that," Newt said, smiling. Then his countenance changed. He stood in front of McAllister with his hands in his pockets, tentative about what he had to say. "You might think this is sort of funny, me asking you this with me not knowing you all that good and all. But you don't really seem like the kind of man who'd be selling whiskey, what with the way you talk and you having read all these books and everything. Course, my papa says even the governor himself likes to take a drink every now and then, and I reckon he's got the best job in the whole state."

McAllister listened patiently, as if the words possessed a certain intuitiveness that he had longed to hear. "That's mighty kind of you to think that, but I don't see whiskey itself as being an evil. If you look in these history books you'll see that whiskey's been a part of civilization since man learned how to make it. It is true that whiskey has ruined a lot of good men, but a lot of good men drink whiskey, in moderation, like Aristotle said."

"Who's that?" Newt asked.

"A Greek fellow. A philosopher. Maybe I'll tell you about him one day."

"Mama's preacher says you got to make a choice between the bottle and the Bible."

"I wish it was that easy," McAllister said. "When I bought this store, the man I bought it from told me that these folks around here would not only count on me for their food and supplies, but they would count on me to provide them good whiskey. It's just like these books. One man can read them and find evil, where another man reads them and finds good."

"What you just said sure makes me feel better. My mama talks about South Carolina all the time. She said her folks had good land up there. She says she misses it something awful, what she calls the low country. Did y'all's folks farm over there?"

McAllister studied the boy's blond hair loose on his forehead and the soft green eyes still holding the question he had asked. "I watched my papa put his whole life into making a living on a piece of poor ground. But I've always believed there is more in the man than there is in the land."

CHAPTER 14

As they rode toward Tarentine's Ferry from Hillsboro, Newt pondered what McAllister had said about there being more in the man than there was in the land. Had he learned it from the books in his office, or had he seen it in the way a man worked his fields? He thought of Earnest Balkum, a man who had sharecropped with his papa for as long as he could remember. Whenever he had passed by the Balkum place, Earnest was always out in his field, either plowing or studying his crop. When he laid his cotton by, the rows were straight and weedless, and Newt had always sensed a rare wisdom in the old man's pace, in the gentle way he handled his undersized mule. He had watched other sharecroppers plow a row, then lean against a shade tree and drink from a bottle of whiskey, their red eyes puzzling toward the gaunt mule and plow as if it were all some strange relic, some hair-and-iron compass that they were somehow obliged to follow. He had seen other sharecroppers muscle against the poorest land in the county with a patience beyond his reckoning, carrying stone after stone to the field's edge in an ancient ritual, each stone an offering, a payment toward some account of miracle.

Jefferson slowed the truck so they could look down over the ferry crossing. "Lord at all them folks."

"They seen us already, too," Newt said. "There's that man, waving his arms at us. That same man you was talking to before we left last Friday."

Jefferson eased the truck down a rut running along the riverbank and stopped in a clearing surrounded by sycamore trees. The people hurried down the path toward the truck in groups of twos and threes, some on foot, some on horses and wagons. Newt

spotted Hap, the man who had been selling the mule the week
before. He was leaning against a tree, whistling a fiddle tune with
all imaginable coolness. A black and tan coon dog tied on a frayed
plow line was curled at his feet. Jefferson climbed into the back of
the truck and uncovered the boxes while Newt sat on the tailgate
of the truck and untied the knot from his burlap bag, ready for
business.

The black farmers converged and huddled around Jefferson
while the mule trader walked straight toward Newt, dragging the
coon dog behind at a reluctant heel. The man was more wiry than
Newt had remembered. The boy could even see the hardness of
his knees, the bone of his shin through his overalls as he walked
toward him. He began talking before he reached the boy, his high,
brisk voice preceding his loose-jointed stride: "Hey. Hey there,
young fella."

The mule trader squatted beside the hound when he got to
Newt, taking a few seconds to hold one ear of the hound in his
palm and smooth his thumb over the coon-scarred ear, pointing
out the worst of the scars to the boy without having to say a word.
His eyes were engaging, uncommonly bright when he looked
toward Newt to speak. "When I caught you out the corner of my
eye last week when I was selling that old gray mule I says to
myself, I says, 'Hap, now that young fella ain't no ordinary run-of-
the-mill boy.' I seen right away you was special. 'Ain't no use in
trying to hide opportunity from that young man,' I says." Hap
held his straw hat reverently in both hands and rocked gently on
his haunches, glancing once toward the sky as if to assure himself
that higher confirmation was available should he need it. "The
man what owned this here hound—God rest his soul—made his
living selling coon hides that this here black-and-tan treed for
him. This here dog done treed so many coons, my friend had to

hire him a little colored boy to go with him at night just to help him tote the coons out."

Hap stood up and twisted his overalls back around to where they fell straight down his front, surveying the landscape behind the boy as if he could see an unexpected and pleasing roll to the land in the distance. "It ain't nothing for this dog to put three coons up one tree. And a mouth? Good morning, mister gentlemens. What you talking 'bout? When this here dog locates down in an old creek bottom, he squalls so loud you'll swear the devil his self done got his foot caught in a bear trap."

Hap brought his voice down to a sanctuary low. "Young fella, I done took a liking to you, and I ain't a man to keep nothing from a body I judge to be of as fine a character as yourself, so I'm fixing to come on across with the gospel of it. I got my eye on a fighting chimp and a cage a man from over at Ellaville's got to sell. He's a older gentleman and said he's just plum give out with it, what with feeding the monkey and counting the money and all. There ain't no more a moneymaking thing in this world that I knows of. Why, that man takes that chimp to county fairs and such and charges folks four dollars a pop to fight him for a chance to win fifty dollars if they can whup it, and young fella, that chimpanzee ain't lost yet. No sir. I seen him fight eight men myself, one right after the other, over in Ellaville last spring, and he whupped all of 'em." Hap cut a sharp eye at the boy. "I reckon you done added up that to being thirty-two dollars clean profit."

Hap took a step closer to the boy and leaned forward, hooking his thumbs into his overall pockets. "Now here's the part you'll like, young fella. That man wants a clean one hundred for the whole outfit and, young friend, I'm short twenty-two dollars. Fact is, I aim to be set up with that chimp for the county fair come Monday." Hap cradled his whiskered chin in the palm of his hand and took on a calculating air, as if to balance the ledger of the situation at hand. "Young fella, I'll tell you what I'm thinking of. I'm thinking hard on sharing my good fortune with you and letting you have this here hound for that same twenty-two dollars."

Newt looked the hound over from tail to ear again before he spoke. "He's a little on the skinny side, ain't he?"

Hap's eyes twinkled, acknowledging the boy's trading skills. "Why, sure, sure he's lean, young fella. I speck you would be too if you was treeing eight or ten coons a night. The widow ain't been a feeding him like she's supposed to, with her being in mourning and all. But this here dog'll catch his own dinner. Just cook up one of them ten coons a night he's a treeing and feed it to him and he'll slick up fancier'n a yellow yard dog."

"I ain't saying he ain't a mighty fine-looking hound besides being a little skinny, mister. But I was thinking he dang near looks too pretty in the face to even want to mess with a coon," Newt said. "If you say he'll tree, I believe it. But I can't use a full-growed dog just yet. I am looking for a good hound pup for my little brother, though. He wants one real bad."

"I'll tell you what I'll do then, young fella. If you's having trouble seeing your way clear to paying me cash for this here hound, then what you say to me swapping him for four bottles of that Sweetwater Branch whiskey? I reckon I could split 'em up in pints, make my twenty-two that away. I don't care for drinking all that much myself. But I always have held a particular liking for trading with folks what did."

"Naw sir, I sure wish I could." Newt reached into his pocket and pulled out a ten-dollar bill. He folded it into squares and then flattened it back out as Hap watched every crease and fold of the bill with great prospect. The boy looked up from the bill, his eyes tactical, calculating. "But I have got an idea that might help you out some. Me and Jefferson, we got some extra money. What would you think about us going in on that fighting chimp with you? That is, if you're willing to take on a partner."

"Whee Lord," Hap blurted out before he could compose himself. Then his veneer transformed immediately, accommodating the proposal with a natural ease, as if he had long known, even expected, that something good was soon going to happen to him. He let the boy's words settle in, allowing the brief silence to solidify their substance. Then he looked upward, shaking his finger gently at the sky as if he could see some specific shape in one particular cloud. "There Ye go. You just keep working in them mysterious ways of Your'n and I'll just keep a saying Amen." Hap then assumed a magniloquent air, shoulders back and chin lifted slightly like a soldier readying himself to be introduced to the commander in chief. He ran his hand down the thigh of his overalls leg and stuck his hand out to the boy. "Young fella, it'd do my heart good to partner up with you."

Newt shook the hand. "I'm Newt Ham, and if my figuring's right this'll make me and Jefferson ten percent owners of the chimp and that rig."

"Your figuring's right, Mr. Newt," Hap acknowledged. "You come to the fair on Monday, and we'll start our settling up then." Hap walked a step closer to the boy and softly tapped the knuckle of his forefinger into the boy's chest with the rhythm of the words he spoke. "You won't be sorry you took in with old Hap Turnipseed. Nosiree, little bobcat tail. A team like me and you? Why, young fella, there ain't no end to what we could do together."

Newt glanced over Hap's shoulder toward Jefferson, who looked as if he had been studying the boy and Hap for a long while. He handed Hap the ten dollars and said, "Well, I guess I best be getting busy. We'll see you on Monday."

Newt watched Hap pull the black and tan hound toward the crowd in the clearing and start a new sales pitch. "Yes sir, mister gentlemens, this here hound is better than being a hired on to Mr. Roosevelt's CCC or WPA or any of the rest of them government programs cause there ain't no waiting in line, ain't no shovels or picks to be a handling, just set this old hound out come dark and collect the coon hides what run to the edge of the tree branch."

Jefferson walked over to Newt and sat next to him on the back of the truck, his face stern. "What you give that white man?"

"Ten dollars. He's fixing to buy a fighting chimp and the cage to go with it, and we're ten percent partners with him."

Jefferson spit the sassafras twig out of his mouth as if it had suddenly soured. "How come you ain't just buy the whole dog for twenty-two?"

"I figured it'd be a better deal to go in on that fighting chimp than owning that hound and hunting him for coon hides. Hap said he never heard of that chimp losing and he aims to charge four dollars a time to fight him. That ought to add up quick."

Jefferson reached in his pocket and felt for his knife, then looked toward Hap in the crowd, glowering his eyes toward him the way a dog marks the boundaries of its yard against a stranger.

Newt stood up and shook the coins in his pocket to get Jefferson's attention. "How many cases we done sold so far?"

"Four and a half," Jefferson answered, turning to face the boy. "They saying Tuggle done cut his price to two dollar a bottle."

Newt leaned into Jefferson's shoulder to whisper in his ear. "You think them folks can tell we watered it some?"

"Naw," Jefferson answered matter-of-factly. "I done told 'em this here was aged shine, that's why she so smooth."

The gray mare appeared out of the woods just as they heard the rustle of the leaves. She was in a slow lope and the man on her back sat tall in the saddle, moving smoothly with her gait. His high-crowned felt hat was floppy and frayed on the edges, and the gray hair falling to his shoulders moved like the horse's mane in the slow lope. His thick, bare forearms held the mare's head steady as he approached. Stopping in front of Newt and Jefferson with an almost imperceptible twitch of the reins, he laid his hands across the saddle horn and then worked the tobacco around in his jaw, turning to spit off to the right before he spoke.

"Well, looky goddamned here. I reckon I done finally found the flow-spout of all the commotion 'round here. So *y'all* are the ones been selling all this bustskull, loop legging all these river-riders round here."

Newt and Jefferson eased closer together, shoulders almost touching, and did not answer. They stared in awe at the man who raised up in his stirrups to spit across his shoulder again, twisting his neck down to wipe his chin on his arm.

"I had two folks fall off'n my ferry last Friday what partook of y'all's corn water," he continued. "Had to stop the dad-blamed ferry mid-river to let my boy fetch 'em back in."

"We sure are sorry about that, mister," Newt offered, taking a half-step forward.

"Name's Tarentine. Sorry? Hellfire, boy," he spit over his shoulder again. "How much y'all getting for that whiskey?"

"Two seventy-five."

"Put two of 'em in my saddle bags, young fella. My boy, he can sell it by the cup to them that's coming from the other side that done sold their corn or cotton. The ones y'all ain't ruined yet," he said, trying to maintain a hard edge in his presence but unable to hold it long before the enthusiasm in Newt's eyes yanked a brief smile out of his closed mouth.

Tarentine reached down in his shirt pocket and pulled the money out. Newt walked up to the gray and put one hand on the mare's neck as Tarentine counted out the money in his other hand.

"Sorry about all them folks, mister," Newt said. "I hope nobody didn't get drowned or nothing."

"Aw, hell, don't you worry none, boy. I got all that took care of. I tell 'em when they get on now, by God, it'll be an extra fifty cent if they fall off and my boy got to fish 'em out. Y'all ain't the only moneymaking sons a bitches round here. If that whiskey's as good as they say, hell, half as good, I'll be needing two bottles ever Friday. I don't reckon nobody'll ever learn to make no good whiskey up here on this end of the river." He flipped his hand in an impatient gesture and then pivoted the gray mare around to lope back from where he had come.

Newt watched until the man and the gray mare finally disappeared down the trail and all that was left was a thin dusting. Jefferson broke the boy's trance. "We best get on to Berner 'fore the mill close."

Newt turned to survey the crowd that was scattered out through the clearing. "I was thinking we could sell all this whiskey right here if we was to stay till sundown. Then we wouldn't have to go way up to Berner this afternoon."

"Naw," Jefferson said. "I done already sent word to Isaac that we coming."

"Well," Newt said with a tentative eye cast up the river road, "long as we can get out of there before they all get good and drunk I reckon it'll be all right."

CHAPTER 15

Driving up the river road toward Berner, Jefferson seemed numb to the jarring, the hard thumps of tires on ruts that occasionally tightened his grip on the steering wheel. He kept his eyes on the road before him as if closing the distance on some thought that he had long struggled to come to terms with. He could hear the drone, the constant chirr of Newt's words, but did not acknowledge the boy's excited talk of the money, the hound, or the fighting chimp. When he reached the sawmill, Jefferson maneuvered the truck around to the side of the building and parked where it could not be seen from the road. He mumbled something as he slid off the seat and out of the truck, but the boy could only distinguish the word "Isaac."

Newt relaxed in his seat and looked out the window. A high-banded cloud slid across the sky like an easy rolling river. He watched the poplar leaves shake in the light breeze against the gray sky. It reminded him of the way a small snag in the river comes alive when the current rises up and bounces it in place. He studied the movement until he began to feel a rising sensation, his mind drifting upward, out of dimension, toward the upside-down river. His thoughts returned once again to his mother, trying to recall if she had ever told him how she met his father in South Carolina. He faced again the question that had become so familiar to him that it no longer seemed as much a question as it did the following of a constant tolling, a single-struck bell, forever echoing through the cold hills: Did it make a difference if he and Addie were born of parents who did not love each other? Sometimes he convinced himself that it did not matter, was simply beyond his control, but as he thought of her now, alone with his papa and Addie, the strap hanging on the nail inside the closet door, he thought that perhaps it did. He remembered the dark bruise on her neck, the harsh purple of it against her white skin. He had glimpsed it when the blue scarf twisted as she sat down at the table, and the boy could tell by the way she looked into his eyes that she knew he had seen it.

The click of the door handle startled him. Jefferson's breathing was quick. "They done seed me. The sheriff, he in there. Talking with Tuggle. I eased on in the mill house and found Isaac, then went straight on out the back."

"You think the sheriff's caught on to what we're doing?"

Jefferson looked back at the building and thought hard. "He looked like he knowed something. I can't say for sure."

"You reckon we ought to go on back to Redbone?" Newt asked.

"Naw." Jefferson took one final look at the sawmill. "Isaac say he coming. He say go on to his house. He'll meet us there come quitting time. I done told him Mr. Earl want us back 'fore dark."

They were parked in the back of Isaac's yard with the rear of the truck tucked in the bushes when they saw Isaac and the crowd of men walking toward them. They searched the faces of the crowd for Red, the man they had left two weeks ago, kneeling with one stiff leg out, his knife now in Jefferson's pocket.

Jefferson stuck the sassafras twig in his mouth dead center and pursed his lips. "If that limping-ass bastard do come, hand that burlap bag here."

Isaac walked straight to the truck and leaned his head into the window. "Who got my money?"

"We got it," Newt said. "We been keeping it for you. Here it is."

Isaac half-glanced at the money as he stuffed it in his pants and looked back over his shoulder at the crowd closing in on them. "How many cases y'all bring?"

"Three and a half," Jefferson said. "Mr. Earl say for us to get three dollar for 'em."

"Damn, y'all high." Isaac staggered back a half step but kept his hands firmly on the open truck window. "Tuggle done cut his price to two dollar."

Newt kept silent while Jefferson stretched up to search the faces in the crowd again.

"Shit," Isaac said. "Y'all gone take care of me?"

Jefferson looked at Newt. "We'll take care of you," Newt confirmed. "Same as before."

Newt and Jefferson got out of the truck, lifted the whiskey from the floorboard, and set it on the grass. Jefferson knelt over the whiskey and opened a bottle. He raised it in both hands, then turned it up high while facing the crowd of men. They studied his face as if he was a preacher in the pulpit, choir silent, and him ready to deliver the first words of his sermon. When he withdrew the bottle, he kept his eyes skyward and blew a high rising moan. "Ooooweee. Lord have mercy, peoples. The Man, He say ask and ye shall receive. That's what the Man say. I say, 'Hands me the money and it will be given you.' That's what *I* say." He handed the bottle to Newt. "Set this here in the front seat for me." The crowd, unsure of how to approach the levity of Jefferson's words, finally followed each other on down, murmuring hard, short phrases as they came. Jefferson bent over the cases, dispensing the bottles and giving the money to Newt. When the bottles were gone, the crowd scattered into small groups throughout the yard.

Isaac walked toward Newt with an open bottle in his hand and a grin on his face like the curled lip of a sardine can. He spoke in a feminine mock. "That woman in that blue dress say, 'Where my sweet little white meat done gone?' You stick your finger in a furry old hole, boy, and a snake liable to bite it," he said, laughing. Then he cocked his head slightly and deepened his voice with a question. "You wanting you some of that dark and salty, ain't you? Yeah. I can see it in them eyes you wanting you some."

A light-skinned man with wavy hair walked over to stand beside Isaac. Newt had not seen him before and could not determine whether the man was white or black. "That woman'll have her way with you, li'l man," he said. "She liable to hold a knife on you till she get satisfied. Can you work good with a knife on you, boy?" The crowd moved closer toward Newt, laughing and shuffling loosely in front of him.

Newt smiled, keeping his head down but his eyes looking up at them from under the brim of his hat. "I reckon I might could figure out what to do with it if I had to."

"Oh Lord. Oh Lord. Listen at him," they howled, shuffling backwards and holding their crotches. "We gone see. She be coming. Then we gone see 'bout that."

Isaac walked over to Newt again, a cocky bounce now in his stride, and stood abreast of him. He spoke out of the side of his mouth to the boy while keeping his eyes on his friends, holding his pinky finger in front of the boy's face. "They wouldn't be nothing left of you but a little old grub worm when that woman get done with you, boy."

Newt kept his head down, shook it from side to side. Jefferson stepped in front of Isaac and stood next to Newt. "We best get on. You drives. I'm fixing to do me some drinking."

Newt steered the truck slowly around the washed-out holes in the road and glanced over at Jefferson, who was holding the bottle between his thighs and turning the bottle cap over and over with his thumb and forefinger.

Jefferson took several long pulls from the bottle, and it started to loosen his tongue. "Making money ain't as hard as all them white folks makes it out to be. All you gots to have is something to sell what folks want real bad. Shit. That's all that is. How much we done made?"

"I ain't had a chance to work all the way through it yet, but I'm guessing we'll make over a hundred dollars without all them extras. When you add up all them extras for cutting it and adding a quarter and fifty cent more for a bottle here and there, we liable to have over a hundred and twenty clean profit, plus the money we came with." Newt, realizing that he had forgotten to mention the ten dollars he had invested with Hap, started to deduct it from his calculations but glanced over at Jefferson and thought better of it.

Jefferson picked up the bottle again and shook it. "It beads up just as good even cut some. Can't hardly taste no difference. Beaucat, he know what he doing."

"What you gonna buy with your money?" Newt asked.

"River bottomland," Jefferson answered.

"What would a good piece of land cost, anyway?" Newt asked.

"'Bout eight dollar an acre for good land, farmland," Jefferson said. "'Bout five dollar for land they done cut through."

"Dog. That means we could buy ten or fifteen acres with the money we already got. Just think if we was to do this for a year how much land we could get. If we worked long enough, why, we could help all these folks around here who want some land to get some. They wouldn't have to count on nobody for nothing then, besides praying every now and then for a little rain."

"I aims to get my fill of it first, 'fore I go off helping folks I don't even know 'bout," Jefferson said, lifting the bottle to his lips to take a more measured sip this time.

Newt was silent for a few moments, then said, "Ain't it funny how sometimes when you feel real good like right now, you're afraid something bad's gonna happen to kind of equal it out 'cause everything just feels too good to be true? It's like when you find something special that you wasn't expecting to find and the very first thing you wonder is 'what am I about to lose to make up for it?' Sometimes in the summer me and Addie and Mama'll be out on the porch watching the lightning bugs or the stars over the fields with everybody being real quiet, feeling just as peaceful as you please, and then we'll see Papa's headlights pulling down the road toward the house."

Jefferson turned to speak, but the boy had already started up again. "Then again, sometimes it happens just the other way. Like late at night when a great big storm blows, it sounds like something with great big old arms is out there tearing the house right out of the ground, flinging the tin off the roof. And it gets louder and louder, and just when you're sure it can't get no worse, all of a sudden you wake up the next morning and everything is just as calm as you please, like there ain't been no storm at all. Sometimes it just don't seem like there's no in between at all, just real real good or real real bad."

"I don't mind losing something if I's to get me twenty acres," Jefferson said, having held the thought ready.

"You could buy fifteen acres with what money we got now, and you already got the best mule around Redbone to boot," Newt said.

"I'd have to get me one more mule with all that land," Jefferson said, his stature erect, looking out across the fields they rode by as if he already owned them. "Ida, she can plow good as me."

"Me and Addie could come over and help y'all sometime. He might not look it, but Addie's real strong in the shoulders. I believe he could catch on to plowing in no time at all."

Newt slowed the truck to look at something far up the road on the edge of the wood's line. At first it appeared to be a large deer bedded down with its head up and then a brown boar hog standing perfectly still, getting ready to bolt across the road. "You see that? Way up the road there?"

Jefferson leaned up in his seat and studied it as they got closer. "That's a man squatting down."

"Dog if it ain't," Newt said. "I can see it now. Looks like something's the matter with him, don't it?"

The man was sitting on the ground at the wood's edge. They could not see his face because his head was down, resting on the arms folded over his knees. The brown round-crowned hat did not move until the truck got within a few yards and stopped. The man lifted his spent eyes in their direction, but they did not seem to focus on either one of them directly.

"You all right, mister?" Newt called out of Jefferson's window.

"Keep on going," Jefferson said, flipping his hand in an impatient gesture.

Newt leaned over Jefferson. "You need a ride, mister? We going to the Redbone crossroads. We can take you that far." The man rose up and looked through the windshield at Newt, then Jefferson. He was tall and gangly with broad shoulders and long arms. His coat was buttoned snugly to the top button, and his hat was pulled down firm on his forehead and slightly cocked to the right, making his smooth brown face visible from the eyes to the chin and back to the ears.

"This here's Jefferson," Newt said. "He works for my papa. I'm Newt."

"I's Carver," the man said, staring down the road.

"Everything all right?" Newt asked again.

The man half-turned toward them but kept looking down the road. "I be all right after while, I reckon."

Newt reached over Jefferson and opened the door and the man got in. Carver looked between Jefferson's legs at the bottle. "You minds if I has me a taste? I needs it bad."

Jefferson acted as if he heard nothing. Newt nudged him with his elbow and Jefferson handed Carver the bottle. Carver put one hand around the throat of the bottle and the other on the bottom and turned it up, swallowing until his mouth, throat, and lungs could take no more, his eyes reddening as if all the heat from the whiskey escaped through them. He took in a deep breath and blew it out as Jefferson snatched the bottle from his hands.

"Lord, Lord." Carver dropped his head toward his lap. "Never even seed it coming."

"What you mean?" Newt asked. "Did something bad happen?"

Carver nodded, head down. "My wife."

"Oh Lord," Newt said. "Is she sick?"

Carver straightened up quickly. "Hell naw. I come home 'fore noon to eat dinner. We was up on the government land cutting wood and I's suppose to be home 'bout dark. But we done got our load and come on back. I walks in the door and I hears something in the bedroom. I eases over to the bedroom door and it's crack open. I looks in and, Lord, Sweet Jesus, a man in there doing my wife in the bed what I done bought and paid for. And she moaning, too, long and slow. I watch 'em for a while 'cause I couldn't move my legs none. She seed me standing in the door and he look up and grab his pants and jump out the window 'fore I could move. Left his shoes and shirt on the floor. Had him a limp, too. I knowed who it was."

"Dog, mister. Seeing your wife with another man, that must of hurt your feelings something awful."

Carver turned away, looking out the window. "Just seeing her in there with another man, that ain't what hurt so bad."

"It ain't?"

"Hell naw. What hurt most was—" He stopped abruptly, eyes closed as if to call the scene back into his mind. "Motherfucker was doing his business better'n I been doing it. I could tell it by how she's moaning."

Newt let go a soft whistle of sympathy. "Lord, mister. What you plan on doing now? Where you headed?"

"Ain't no way of knowing for sure." He reached in his coat pocket, pulled out a large case pocketknife, and opened the hooked blade. He started working it under his fingernails and stopped to test its sharpness by rubbing his thumb across the edge.

Out of the corner of his eye, Jefferson watched the man work the blade. He set the bottle between him and Newt and pulled his knife from his overall pocket, opening it to its longest blade. "I knows what you talking," Jefferson said, pulling the point of the knife across his thumbnail. "This here knife done got me three years on the chaingang for getting drunk and cutting a man. I didn't intend to kill nobody. 'Fore I knowed it, he was layed out on the floor."

"What'd you cut him for?" Carver said, suddenly alert, watching Jefferson work his knife.

"Said something made me mad," Jefferson answered. "He pull out a knife on me acting the fool. Sure didn't 'tend to kill him though. Naw sir, sure didn't 'tend to kill him."

"Don't make no never mind to me if they's to put me on the chaingang. All the same to me," Carver said, looking out the window with an indignant jut to his jaw. "All the same to me."

"You ain't really thinking about killing nobody are you, mister?" Newt asked.

"Look like I ain't got no say in it. Else move on. All them folks be laughing 'hind my back."

"They's plenty of other women up there, ain't they, mister?" Newt asked. "My mama says they're like fish in the sea."

"Not like this 'un," Carver said, pursing his lips down at the blade as he ran it across the outside of his thumbnail. "I couldn't bring myself to cut this 'un. It'd be like cutting my own self. Naw, it's got to be him."

"Me and Jefferson was just talking 'bout how when a real bad thing happens then most times a real good thing happens right after the bad."

"Can't no good come from this here, child," Carver said. He took one more look at the knife in Jefferson's hand as if to remeasure its length, then folded his own blade shut and slid it back in his coat pocket.

"I can tell them folks ain't having no fun on that chaingang," Newt said. "You hardly ever see 'em smiling when you pass by 'em on the road. They always looking up at you like they wish you would carry 'em off with you. Them chains look mighty hard to work in, too."

Newt slowed the truck to a stop at the crossroads. "This is the place we got to turn off, mister." Carver got out of the truck, closed the door, and looked down toward Redbone.

"Wait a minute, mister," Newt said, reaching over Jefferson again. "Here. Take this two dollars. Maybe you can buy something that'll take your mind off things for a while, long enough to let something good start happening again."

Carver took the money and looked at Jefferson, then backed into the dark where they could not see him.

Newt let the clutch out and headed for Beaucat's. He turned toward Jefferson with a somber expression. "I ain't never heard you killed nobody."

"Ain't." Jefferson rolled the sassafrass twig in his mouth as if amused with the thought. "Just making sure he put that knife back in his pocket."

CHAPTER 16

Sheriff Wills cupped the glare off the window as he looked into Sonny Tuggle's office. Sonny sat at a small table, working over a spread of papers. The heel of his right foot was cocked off the floor as he worked, and he rocked his toes against the floor like a schoolboy working through a word problem. The sheriff rapped twice on the door.

"Come on in, Clarence." Tuggle half-turned, eyes rolling at the sheriff over low-hung glasses. He hovered back over the papers. "Give me a minute or two to finish figuring up this payroll. This is giving me one hell of a headache."

"Go ahead on," the sheriff said. "I ain't in no hurry." Sheriff Wills wandered around the room, stopping to look at the photographs along the wall. He studied the picture of Tuggle's father, his hard eyes intent on something in the distance as he led a pair of gray mules over snow-covered ground. The mules were hitched to a wagon full of turpentine barrels in a stand of virgin longleaf. The tin cups hanging from the center of the gashed trees to collect turpentine made the forest look like a drove of armless beggars, frozen in their long brown coats.

The sheriff glanced over his shoulder occasionally to see if Tuggle had finished his work. At fifty-six, Sonny had accumulated an even spread of soft bulk over his body, but his big frame managed to carry the extra weight as if it were no burden at all. His high forehead held the lineless quality of a man who had not much documented his worries, and his oversized ears with their fleshy lobes gave him a curiously friendly, accessible look. His mouth and chin possessed the smooth, unseasoned quality of a man who neither drank nor took tobacco, perhaps out of sound choice, but more likely due to a tentative nature toward chance itself. At times he seemed too easily content, domesticated almost, as if he had gradually acquired the traits of his four daughters and his wife rather than carrying on those of the man in the photograph.

Tuggle's father had started the lumber business in Berner in 1886 and had made most of his money shipping lumber and turpentine on the railroad to Savannah. Sonny Tuggle had kept the business running more out of inertia than ambition. If it had not been for his sense of obligation to the men who worked for him and to his wife, his four daughters, and their families, he would have shut the mill down long ago to work the thirty-acre river-bottom field his father had left him. Sonny had lost most of the cash money he had inherited from his father keeping the mill open during the worst of the Depression, and he still could not account for where or exactly when it had gone.

Whereas no one had dared cross the old man Tuggle, Earl Ham had shown up from South Carolina twelve years ago and gradually taken his share of business from the son. Sonny had never actually seen it happen nor had he intended to let it happen. One day it had simply appeared as fact, the way brush gradually creeps into the edge of a field until it becomes a full-blown thicket too dense to plow under.

In the summer of '26 Sonny sat down with Earl to agree on the territories of their lumber and whiskey business. Although a deal was made, Sonny had known that it would only be a matter of time before his rival would overstep. His father had left him a simple code of conducting business: "I can get along with any man until he gets in my pocket." But the son knew little of what to do when that code was tested.

Sonny was regarded as a fair man, paying his workers a good wage and taking care of their families in times of trouble. Yet there was one paradox that always loomed, that of actual pedigree handed down from the grandfather through the father to settle in Sonny like the same thin whiskey he now sold. The people in town had seen the temper only twice: once in his thirties when Sonny rode his bay gelding into the courthouse to get his help out of jail and once in his forties when he would have beaten a man to death with his bare hands in the lumberyard had the other workers not pulled him off. Sonny never said why he had done it, but from that day on the townsfolk spent a great deal of time speculating on the exact degree of Sonny's breaking point.

Sonny removed his glasses and swiveled his chair around to face the sheriff. He rubbed his eyes for a long while as if they were tired not only from the numbers he was working, but just plain tired.

"Earl Ham." He spoke the words with neither inflection nor complaint, but more as if it were a common saying, its meaning known to all. "I guess we knew this day was coming."

"Oh, it's sure been coming, all right," the sheriff said. "Earl's done finally went and dropped his plow in the off-row, ain't he?"

Tuggle blew an impotent sigh, a faint whistling through his parted lips. "It's bad enough him selling whiskey to our own hands. Now they're saying he's cutting us out at the ferry crossing."

"That ain't the hide, hair, and guts of it, neither," the sheriff said. "They say Earl's boy and Jefferson was over at Hillsboro last Friday. Folks seem to think he's selling whiskey through that new store-keep from South Carolina, McAllister."

"Hillsboro?" Tuggle repeated slowly as if trying to reconcile the name with the place. "How much they selling in Hillsboro?"

"Aw hell, that's hard to say with them tightlipped folks in that county." The sheriff swung his head from side to side. "But once they get 'em a toehold, there won't be no stopping 'em."

"I cut the price to two dollars last week," Tuggle offered.

"Yeah, I heard," the sheriff said, an apologetic trailing to his voice. "But that ain't gonna make no difference, Sonny. The problem is, we ain't got nobody that can make whiskey worth a shit no more. Hell, I can't hardly bear to drink it my own self. Folks around here been bad-mouthing it for I don't know how long, saying it tastes like horse piss with the foam farted off it."

"I'm working on it," Tuggle said. "I hired a man out of Indian Springs. We might just have to set him up on Falling Creek for a while if it comes to it." Sonny stood up and pointed feebly toward the chair across from his desk. "I told that bastard—he was setting right there in that chair—'I'll stay out of Redbone if you'll stay out from up here.' Earl stood up, shook my hand on it, and me knowing all along you couldn't trust that cigar-eating son of a bitch."

"I could pick up Earl's boy and Jefferson next time they come up here," the sheriff said, a grin curling up his left cheek. "Take 'em in to the jailhouse and scare 'em up some."

"Naw hell, that wouldn't do no good. He'd just find somebody else to send. I figure Earl to be like an old hard-to-catch mule Papa had one time, running around all high-headed, its nose up in the air, too fancy to watch where it's going. Papa looped a noose around the meat of that mule's tail, then stretched it under its belly and tied it to the halter. He pulled it so tight that mule couldn't see nothing but its own belly and tail. Left him roped up like that for three days. But from then on, that mule kept the best head-set in the lot. Papa could train anything."

"If you waiting on me, you backing up, boss," the sheriff said, shuffling back a step. "Shit. I been ready. If we aim to do it, let's go on and do it right. Be done with it. You just say the word, Sonny, and I'll get Red to go on down there and take care of business. Hell, that big sombitch'll get Earl's head set right. Come out the canebreak or something and go to snatching his ass around like he's an overgrowed sissy. Hell, Earl's liable to shit right there in his old big-ass britches."

Sonny did not smile. "Naw. Red might get carried away and kill him."

"Yeah, I reckon Red is prone to get carried away," the sheriff agreed, rubbing his chin. "I tell you what I could do. I could send my new deputy on down there, Eugene Raintree. That boy's from the mountains, and built like a damn big old bear. He's a tough 'un, too, that boy. I could get him to go on down there and rough Earl up real good, and Earl don't even know who he is. Now, old Eugene ain't gonna go bowlegged toting his brains, Sonny. I'll give you that, but he'll do just what I tell him, by God."

Sonny listened to the sheriff with a dense eye, as if resorting the phrases the sheriff had spoken into an order he could understand.

"Come on, Sonny. Let me send Eugene on down there. He'll do just what I say do and won't say nothing to nobody. We ain't got to worry 'bout that. Hell, he'll stick a corncob up Mr. Highfalutin's ass and spoon feed him castor oil if that's what I tell him to do."

Sonny's boyish mouth pursed briefly sour. He looked over to the wall of photographs and studied for a moment the one of his father leading the two mules. "I reckon he would have put an end to it a long time ago." Sonny turned from the picture with a hard look of his own. "Just make damn sure you get it done right this time. You take that Eugene with you next Saturday and follow Earl out to where he gets his whiskey on Sweetwater Branch. Take one of these trucks around here and don't neither of you wear a uniform. Earl will know we're behind it without us having to advertise. Drop Eugene off and then go on up the road, hide the truck in the woods, and wait for him. He'll have to rough him up good now. Learning don't come natural to Earl. You tell Eugene to make damn sure Earl comes out of that ass-whupping knowing one thing and knowing it good—if he sells so much as one sliver of his whiskey up here again, over to Hillsboro, or even at Tarentine's Ferry, there won't be no more warnings. Somebody'll find his big ass floating in that river. Don't let Eugene take no gun, now. I'm too damn wore out to be dealing with a killing."

"That big old boy won't need no gun," the sheriff said, eyes beetling with the thought. "He'll take care of it just like you said, Sonny. I'll see to it."

CHAPTER 17

Jefferson had promised to pick up the boy early that Monday morning to go to the county fair. Newt sat on the front porch and listened for the first rattle of the truck, but the last few seconds of darkness seemed to refine a peculiar stillness out of the fields around him, and for a long moment it seemed nothing on earth dared draw a breath. As first light came, a small flock of sparrows appeared, pulsing through the air like a metronome before dropping into the field. They fed a few seconds and lifted up to fly toward the wood line, navigating their direction in a loose, yet symphonic pattern, each wing and tail pushing or pulling some part of the flock's rudder.

Earl had not come home the evening before, and Naomi had been relaxed and talkative as she sat with her boys by the fire, recalling the stories of all the places their grandfather had seen when he worked for the railroad. Newt tried to imagine the Ozarks the way she described them, the dark, timbered hills and all the game they must have held, the long train steaming over the Mississippi River with his grandfather waving at riverboat captains and gamblers. She told them about the trip to New Orleans she had taken as a young girl. The way she described the mansions of St. Charles Avenue, the sounds of the trumpets on Bourbon Street, and the Creole women made the boy wonder if it all must have been made by some other hand, some other creator entirely. The lights of Jefferson's truck flickered once through the tree line, then reappeared, moving straight toward him as if the boy willed their direction the way the birds had done theirs. He felt a strange, yet elemental calm in the power of the lights approaching, the two powerful eyes suspended in the blue dawn.

Later, Newt and Jefferson were working their way through
the crowd at the ferry crossing when they heard Hap's voice down
by the river, his whine scaling the high notes of his range. "Fifty
dollars cash to the man that can pin this here chimp."

Newt shook Jefferson's shoulder as they hurried through the
crowd. "What'd I tell you? That's Hap up there. And see that
chimp in that cage? We own part of it."

"Just five dollars'll get you fifty. What you say, mister
gentlemens? Five dollars for fifty, just for pinning something that
ain't no bigger'n a school boy to the floor of that cage for three
seconds. I got the Reverend Banks, who's passing through from
Alabama, here to do the counting." Hap pointed to the small man
with horn-rimmed glasses dressed in a hasty black outfit, the
frayed white shirt collar turned out to effect a circuit preacher.
"He's a man of the Lord, ladies and gentlemen. Ain't no need to
worry about fair play." Hap strutted back and forth in front of the
crowd, his stretched neck and pointed straw hat with the long
feather punctuating the rhythm of his pitch. "I reckon y'all might
of been a hearing, and it is a fact, that this here chimp, old Abe,
ain't been pinned down in quite a spell. But friends, the whole
truth of it is, he's been a scuffling with city folks mostly. He ain't
been against no real men, sawyers and farmers such as yourself, in
a considerable spell. He might not have the edge that he's been a
use to having so I'm gonna ask the first man if he'd be so kind as
to be a little easy on old Abe the first go round. Who'll be the first
to take him on?" Hap pulled a roll of bills out of his pocket and
teased the crowd with it like a half-apple to a mule. "Who'll be the
first to take home this here fifty dollars cash money?"

The cage, roughly the size of a large cotton wagon, was
enclosed on all four sides and the top with iron bars. The chimp
swung leisurely from the top bars of the cage, eyeing the
onlookers with a distant calm, as if endowed with a supreme

confidence. As Hap pitched for the first contestant, the chimp hopped flatfooted to the floor and bared all his teeth in a lip-parting smile, putting one finger on the top of his head to fully identify himself as the one worthy of all the commotion. When fully upright, the chimp stood no more than five feet and weighed only 125 pounds.

Jefferson half-turned to Newt without taking his eyes off the chimp. "I believes I can whup something ain't no bigger'n that."

"What you mean?" Newt asked. "You ought not to be wanting to whup something we own part of. What makes you think you can pin that thing anyway when Hap just said he ain't been took down in so long?"

Jefferson dug the sassafras twig behind his eyetooth, studying the poses of the chimp the way he would have sized a plow mule for purchase. "I gots it in mind to pin it right quick, get that fifty. That ten dollars worth'll still be ours when I gets done."

"Good Lord," Newt said, turning a circle to gather his thoughts before he spoke again. "I sure wouldn't go in there first if I was you. Let's watch that thing fight a few other folks and see how it goes about whupping 'em."

Newt moved closer to the cage to study the moves of the chimp like a trainer scouting for his prizefighter. No one stepped forward quick enough to suit Hap, so he sweetened the proposition. "Four dollars," he called out, slapping his thigh. "Four dollars for the first man who'll try old Abe."

Out stepped Buford Oxley, a well-known sawyer who had cut and hauled wood for Sonny Tuggle for more than fifteen years. At six feet four, his broad shoulders possessed that rare quality of staying up high and square even as he stood relaxed. His forearms, when flexed, were as thick as Newt's thighs. Without taking his eye off the chimp, Buford handed his hat to his wife, a wiry woman who stood only a few inches taller than his waist, and emptied his tobacco and other pocket belongings into it. Buford counted four dollars into Hap's hand.

"Whee, Lord!" Hap rocked back on his heels. "And a fine-looking man we got for our first contestant, ladies and gentlemen. Ain't but the one rule, neighbor—take your boots off. It wouldn't be fair to old Abe if you was to kick him with hard boots on with him being barefooted and all."

Buford leaned against the cage to take off his boots, handing them to his wife who cradled them in her arms along with the hat as if boots not worn should not touch the ground. He rolled up his sleeves and stood waiting. When Hap opened the cage door, the chimp Abe cocked his head slightly to the side and narrowed the slits of his eyes in a playful, mocking anger. The chimp measured out his front feet squarely on the floor and bristled a small clump of hair between his shoulder blades. He then pursed his lips as if to whistle, but instead launched a high treetop squall, so shrill that it silenced every murmur in the crowd. Buford, ignoring the high shriek, walked into the cage and spread his arms out wide, like a grizzly bear in pursuit of a wounded prey. The chimp, reassuming his previous calm demeanor, hopped from one side of the cage to the other, holding on by one arm and occasionally glancing over his shoulder to check his opponent's position. Buford inched forward in confident, measured steps, stalking the chimp toward one corner of the cage. As if long accustomed to this tactic, Abe allowed Buford to work him into a corner, then the chimp hunkered down on all fours, low to the ground. When Buford made his final lunge, the chimp sprang straight up in the air and grabbed the iron bars on the top of the cage. Then, with the dexterity of a trapeze artist, the chimp swung his body completely around and with both feet flat out, kicked Buford squarely in the shoulders all the way to the back rails of the cage, sending him to slither down the cage bars like an over-easy egg moved from a sideways frying pan to the plate. Buford's wife squalled much like the chimp had done to start the match, still cradling the boots to her bosom. Two men dressed like Buford in round-topped felt hats with the brims flung down like oversized funnels came into the cage and helped carry Buford out. Hap went behind the cage and fed the chimp something from his pockets.

Newt moved shoulder to shoulder with Jefferson. "Good godalmighty," he said, turning a circle again. "You see how fast that thing done that? That thing put a hurting on that man. You ain't still thinking about going in there, are you?"

Jefferson nodded, studying the chimp and rolling up the sleeves of his flannel shirt.

"Ain't no real hurry, is it?" the boy reasoned. "Let's watch another one before you try it."

Hap had begun calling for the next contestant before he got back to the front of the cage. "That fella ain't hurt, ladies and gentlemen. That there fella was just so doggone big he got old Abe a little worked up. That's all it is. He's got some of his spunk wore off now. I'll guarantee you that. Who'll be the man to do it? Five dollars for a chance to pin this monkey'll get you fifty if you win." Hap stopped to crack open one of the peanuts he had remaining in his hand and sucked the meat out of the hull. "Who's the next bravest fella in the bunch?"

"Will he bite?" a man asked from the crowd.

Hap looked through the crowd to find who had spoken and addressed the man directly. "Friend, I sure hope you don't figure me to be the kind to put no biting animal against a human creature. This here chimp's been taught better'n that. He ain't never bit before that I knows of. Just to show you how sure I am old Abe wouldn't do such a thing, I'll pay twenty out if he so much as nips at a body." Hap looked over his shoulder and studied the chimp for several seconds, as if hoping the chimp could understand at least part of what he had just said.

Jefferson leaned toward Hap, but before he could make his move, Ned Ussery, a black sharecropper from Redbone, had already stepped up to Hap with the five dollars counted out and ready to hand over. Ned stood at no more than five feet eight, but his compact frame was all bone and muscle. By the look on his clinched jaw, the roll of money Hap used to tease the crowd was soon to be his. Ned was known to be an agreeable sort, less prone to fight than ready to smile, so the crowd buzzed its surprise as he counted out the bills into Hap's hand.

As Ned entered the cage, the chimp, rather than give forth his high-pitched squall, folded his arms at his chest and leaned back against the rail much like a man would pose if he was waiting at the terminal for the arrival of a train. He then bared his front and bottom teeth, again by the stretched and exaggerated parting of his lips, and shook his head from side to side toward the crowd, mocking them for the challenger they had sent forth.

Ned tried a different strategy than the first contestant. When Hap closed the door behind him, Ned immediately hung one of his muscular arms down to the floor and shuffled around three-legged, imitating the chimp's rapid honking as he went. The chimp folded his lip-parting smile and retreated to the corner, pushing the loose skin of his head down over his forehead as he studied the finer points of Ned's imitation. Without making eye contact with old Abe, Ned kept enlarging a pattern of figure eights, stealing closer and closer to the chimp with each loop and making sure that his back was to the chimp each time he passed. As Ned approached what was to be his last pass, he glanced over his shoulder to exact the chimp's position and thrust his elbow squarely into the chimp's throat. The weight of Ned's momentum when he threw the elbow sent the chimp somersaulting to the back rails. Old Abe managed to regain his balance at the end of the roll, and he got up as if it were all one intended motion. At full speed, the chimp ran squalling one time around the cage, then scaled the side rails to the top, where he perched with his hand on his throat, dead still and now silent, eyeing his prey. Ned, sensing a chance to finish off the chimp, lunged upward to grab a dangling ankle, but the chimp quickly pulled himself out of reach and, again like a trapeze artist, swung his body around to catch Ned squarely against the chest with both heels, even harder this time as if to compensate for the slip punch Ned had given him earlier. The kick caught Ned, who was standing completely upright, so squarely at the top of his short frame that instead of sending him back against the rails, it flattened him on the floor. Old Abe followed him down to the ground so quickly that it looked as if his feet were still attached to Ned's shoulders. Without looking at the limp black hulk beneath him, the chimp touched his left foot on Ned's stomach and, again, put his forefinger on the top of his head and turned a small circle, self-proclaiming victory in his now familiar lip-parting smile.

"Lord a mighty," someone cried out. "Reckon which one of 'em was the real gorilla?"

As they carted the man out of the cage, Jefferson took off his boots and stepped forward out of the crowd toward Hap without hesitation. He counted the money into Hap's hand while Hap studied him with a strained hint of recognition, finally looking over to find Newt in the crowd. He smiled at the boy and winked.

Jefferson felt a hand on his shoulder as he stepped up to the door to enter the cage; he turned as Newt pulled him a few feet over to the side and said, "I believe I figured out something about the way that thing moves that can help you out some."

Jefferson bent closer to Newt's mouth, keeping his chest still bowed and shoulders straight to avoid compromising the proud posture of what he was about to do. "Go on in there like that first man done," Newt said. "Like a bear stalking something and work him in the corner real slow. When you get him worked in the corner, lunge at him, but don't really go after him, just make him think you are. That'll make him spring up and grab the top bars and swing his self around with those heels of his coming flat out towards you. Now when he does that, you crouch all the way to the ground as fast as you can get there and as low as you can go, and he'll miss you with them heels. Then, all you gotta do is spring up real quick, grab him by the ankles, and yank him down to the floor. When he hits the ground, jump on top of him and pin him. I'm thinking he'll be so shook up he won't know what hit him."

Jefferson, having listened intently to what the boy was saying, walked into the cage, glancing back at Newt as Hap shut the door behind him. Newt gave him a nod of confidence.

"I know this here fella," Hap said, raising his hand toward the cage. "He ain't afraid of nothing, 'specially no little old sassy monkey."

Jefferson entered the cage and took the sassafras twig out of his mouth, carefully placing it in the top pocket of his overalls as if it were a gold toothpick. He spit on his hands and, rubbing them together, bent his knees and extended his arms out in the same manner of the first contestant, inching toward Abe. At first, the chimp did not even bother to look at the new contestant, his eyes searching the top of the cage in apparent boredom. As Jefferson worked to within a yard, the chimp cut his eyes toward him sharply, their cool intent seeming to dare Jefferson to step closer. But when Jefferson made his final lunge, the chimp jumped in one leap to the top rails of the cage, where he quickly completed his trapeze-like twist and, turning around with both feet flat out, dug his heels toward Jefferson in a hard-driving swing, the nail of his big toe gashing across Jefferson's cheek as he ducked to the ground. The chimp seemed to hesitate in mid-air, the momentum of his not catching Jefferson squarely leaving his body suspended for a moment and perpendicular with the ceiling. As the chimp started his downswing from this position, Jefferson sprung up out of his crouch, grabbed the chimp by his ankles, and yanked down with all his strength. The chimp, pleading on the way down with an unnerving, demonic scream, landed squarely and silently on his back. Jefferson followed him to the ground, throwing his body firmly over the chimp's chest and spreading his arms and legs wide to leverage further the strength of his position.

The roar of the crowd hushed as Abe hit the ground and Hap rushed to the cage door. The reverend, caught off-guard by the sudden call to duty, looked toward Hap for instructions while the crowd jeered at him to count. Adjusting his makeshift collar as if to loosen his throat for speaking, he looked toward the sky. "Lord Jesus one," he started in a slow reverential appeal. "Lord Jesus two," he seconded, hands clasped and eyes closed, and then, widening his arms above his head as if to part the sea, finally came forth with the conclusion, "Lord, Lord have mercy three," to which the crowd whooped and cheered its approval.

Hap ran into the cage as Jefferson rose off the chimp, still semi-crouched as he took a step back, ready for a fresh assault should the chimp rise. Hap bent down over the chimp, shaking its shoulder as he put his ear to the chimp's loose outstretched lips.

"That fella done knocked your gorilla silly," someone shouted from the crowd.

"See if you can hire that man what done knocked him out for your new gorilla," another chimed in.

Hap placed his hand on the chimp's chest to feel his heart and, again, bent down to put his ear to the chimp's lips. Newt rushed inside the cage and squatted beside Hap.

"He's dead," Hap whispered.

"Maybe he's just got all the breath knocked out of him," Newt answered.

"Naw, Mr. Newt. He's dead," Hap said, pinching the chimp's brow back to take one last look into its eyes. "Grab his legs and let's take him out of here. Ain't no need to let these folks be gawking all over him."

Newt grabbed the chimp around the legs, and Hap held up the loose torso from under the chimp's armpits. They hauled the sagging body out of the cage with Jefferson following like a man still stalking his prey. They took him to Hap's tent that was set up a few hundred feet away and laid him out on the bedroll.

Newt held one of the chimp's curled-up toes between his thumb and forefinger and glanced over to Hap, who had taken off his straw hat and dropped to his knees beside the chimp. "I can't help feeling like it's all my fault," the boy said. "I told Jefferson how I thought he ought to grab him and yank him down and all. I never would of dreamed that would of killed the little fella. And here we was partners in on it, too."

"Aw. Ain't nobody to blame, Mr. Newt. I reckon his time was up, is all. I can't say I ever figured to have to pay out on him, though. Never figured old Abe to lose."

"I reckon it's about as bad as losing a friend, ain't it?" Newt asked.

"Well, I reckon I had done took somewhat of a liking to it. But that monkey'd done got so uppity, winning so many fights when that other fella had him that I couldn't hardly make him mind me no ways. Truth be told, I ain't had him but the two days, and I could already see who was fixing to run this here show. Anytime he'd want something to eat, why he'd just go to hissing at me and show them old bad teeth of his. I said he wouldn't bite none so the folks wouldn't be scared and all, but one time when he was acting up real bad I slapped him on his hiney—like you woulda done a kid that was throwing a fit—and he hauled off and bit me good right here on the arm. Looked like to me he done had it in his eye to put a whipping on me any day now. Yes sir, it was sure a coming."

Hap looked over the chimp again from head to toe. "Don't let nobody tell you they won't eat no meat. That'n there could smell a ham hock a half a mile away."

Hap turned away from the chimp and addressed Newt and Jefferson directly. "I'll sell everything I got to pay y'all if I have to. Y'all don't worry none about that. Y'all won it fair and square and I'll get it to you someway, somehow."

Hap pulled the roll of bills out of his pocket and showed it to Newt. "I knowed it appeared like I had a heap of money in this here roll, but it ain't nothing but a wad of paper rolled up in a couple of one dollar bills." Hap hung his head a little. "It took everything I had, Mr. Newt, to buy this old chimp and cage."

Jefferson, having relaxed his guard, came over to kneel by the chimp with Newt. The boy let him settle beside him before he addressed Hap. "What you figuring on doing with him?"

Hap stood up at Newt's question and worked his hat down snugly on his head. "Well, young fella, it's kind of coming to me as we speak. But knowing you two to be business-minded fellas who knows opportunity when they see it, I reckon ain't no harm in trying it out on you.

"A few evenings back two fellas was passing through and stopped at my camp. Them old boys got to talking bout flying saucers and folks what lived in 'em. Aliens is what them fellas called 'em. They told me about some folks up north of here what found a big burned-out circle in their pasture. Now the wife of the farmer what owned the place, said she caught a glimpse of one of 'em skedaddling through the woods. Well sir, I asked them gentlemen what they suspected 'em to look like, these here aliens, and they said that this here woman said that they was short, dark-skinned, had long arms, funny shaped heads and no hair on 'em."

"Good Lord," Newt said. "No hair at all?"

"Not nary a hair on its body, Mr. Newt, head or nothing, is what they said. Well that night, after them fellas left, I went to check in on old Abe before I went to bed. I shined that kerosene lamp in there, and he was sprawled out on his back just about like he is now, sleeping just as quiet and pretty as you please. Well sir, I got to studying on him and I said to myself, I says, 'Hap. If you was to take the hair off that old chimp he'd look just like that alien them folks was talking about.' And I ain't thought nothing else about it till now, when I seed old Abe sprawled out like he was on that night. Now I reckon it to be a sign of some kind.

"Time's short, Mr. Newt, with old Abe in the state he's in, so I'll tell you what I'm a thinking. I say we shave that monkey clean, every last stitch of hair off his hide. He's bound to look like one of them aliens then, and we'll charge folks to see him, sell tickets. We'll be partners again. I figure we could get him on over to Macon tomorrow and charge folks at least fifty cents apiece to see him."

Newt looked over the chimp again, trying to imagine the clean-shaven features, from the curled bare toes to the crooks and crevices of the animal's loose-skinned head. Jefferson, sassafras twig back in his teeth and a red bandana against his clawed jaw, pondered the outcome of the shaving, moving shoulder to shoulder with Newt to study the form.

Newt shook his head from side to side, still sizing up the chimp. "He dang sure would be a strange-looking thing if you was to shave him clean." He turned to address Hap directly. "If you're planning on shaving him clean and that includes below the waist, then I'm thinking you'll need to wrap something around that part, maybe even something real colorful to make him look like one of those real short African princes or something. I don't think most folks would care to see that part as clean shaven as the rest, especially the women folks."

Jefferson grunted his approval.

"I believe you've got something there, Mr. Newt. I got a rag off an old red velvet blouse I found washed up on the riverbank. We could trim it up and make it fit around him. Then all we'll need is a box deep enough to hold him and some ice to lay under him so he'll keep a few days. If we could just get him down to Macon by noon tomorrow we ought to be able to sell some tickets. If y'all could gather up the box, I'll spend the night shaving old Abe clean and fixing up them red drawers. It's cool enough for him to keep till morning. We can buy some ice to put under him as soon as we get to Macon."

Hap, bobbing his head as if he became more pleased with the idea the more he talked about it, turned to Newt with one eye squinted, the other twinkling as he spoke. "Here's what I'm a thinking. I'll give you boys the first fifty we make, seeing as how I owe your friend that anyway for licking old Abe fair and square. Then we'll split everything fifty-fifty, right down the middle."

"What if folks don't believe it?" Newt asked. "That he's from out in space."

"You just leave that up to old Hap. It ain't no different than selling a hound that won't tree or a mule that won't plow. Them folks'll see what they wanna see, and I'll see to it that they's seeing an alien."

Newt turned to Jefferson. "We in, ain't we?"

Now holding the bandana on his cheek like a poultice, Jefferson removed it and checked it for blood. Then he pulled the sassafras twig from the tight clinch of his teeth, unhinging his jaw so he could speak. "If you's to give me that fifty dollars for whupping it," he said, pointing the sassafrass twig at the chimp, "then we gots us a deal."

"There ain't nothing I'd rather do, friend, than to oblige you on that, but the fact is I ain't got it on me. But you got Hap's word. You'll get your money one way or another. We'll make so much money tomorrow, partner, you'll plum forget what I owed you today. Y'all be here the crack of dawn and we'll get started." Hap rubbed his hands together as if ready to sit down to a feast, the familiar twinkle reset in his eye.

shuffled their hands toward her, giving her encouragement to go inside the tent. Reluctant but caught up in the urging of the crowd, she followed Hap to the tent where he turned the flap open and made a courtly gesture for her to enter. Jefferson stood at the head of the homemade casket with his folded arms low at his midsection to make certain the badge could be seen. The woman inched closer to the casket with her hand at her throat, knees slightly bent and crouched as if creeping to lift a chicken egg out of a place where she knew snakes sometimes hid. With a stiff and regal formality, Jefferson slowly slid the sheet back, first to the chimp's feet, then through the red waistcloth and finally to the glistening torso and bare, sparse-haloed head.

The woman shielded her eyes and opened her mouth round. She blew, "wah-wah-wah," like a train whistle rising in pitch. Her chest then heaved in short uncontrollable spasms until she finally managed the one long breath, and it came out at the end of that, the one, pleading "Help me, Jesus." She then doubled over, hands on her knees, and let out a long curdling moan from deep within in an attempt to rid her body of what she had just witnessed. Hap ran over to hold the woman up as she staggered back a step.

Outside the tent the crowd cocked their eyes toward the sound like a pack of stray dogs pinpointing a deer bleat. The woman exited the opening half-bent with Hap leading her out by her arm to hold her up. Her bottom lip quivered and she suddenly sucked both lips inside of her mouth, making the buckteeth mysteriously disappear. Looking up to the sky, she fanned her face with a white handkerchief in one hand and waved the other toward the sky like one touched at a tent revival. Her lips reappeared fully moistened. "Forgive me, Jesus. For I knows not what I seen."

Some of the crowd rushed around her to ask questions while the rest pushed toward Newt to get in line. "Just pay your half dollar to this young fella as you walk in," Hap said. "One at a time, no touching of the alien. We ain't sure what it's made of. We wouldn't want nobody to get sick. Children is half price. God bless the little children." Hap found Jambo in the crowd to give him a wink.

By two o'clock, more than three hundred people had watched Jefferson pull the white sheet ceremoniously off the clean-shaven chimp. Hap recognized one of the last ones to enter the tent as the sister of the woman who had taught him the death pose. He moved closer to the woman as she knelt by the coffin and placed both palms on it as if feeling for some vibration. She rose with her hands over her eyes and nose, and, in tones that seemed to echo up from a grave, she turned to Hap and said, "Mister. That ain't no alien from out of space. That's the devil his self. Old satan."

At that, the preacher who had spoken earlier broke into the front of the crowd again and urged, "Listen, my people. You don't want to look on the face of the devil. You could go blind. Leave this tent and go to your homes." Hi voice quivered like the liquid trembling of a hoot owl.

The blacks ran first, most of them screaming, followed by the whites, who were just as frantic and wide-eyed yet attempted to maintain some semblance of dignity as they scurried along. Ten or twelve remained, lingering around the tent as if drugged, mesmerized by their own inability to leave.

A small red-cheeked man, middle-aged in a ragged tweed suit with his thumbs tucked into his vest pockets, approached Hap. "My friend, have you considered stuffing that alien? I'm a taxidermist by trade. We might be able to sell him to famous institute, a museum of some kind. I'd be willing to take on such a negotiation for you. The normal fee for such a transaction would be ten percent of the gross proceeds."

"That's mighty kind of you to ask, neighbor, but I can't oblige. The Lord's done spoke to us on this subject. We aim to get him over to Ellaville for a proper burying. The same way we'd want done if we was to get lost up yonder somewheres." Hap flipped his hand up toward the stars.

"Hey mister." A man with thick glasses appeared from behind the tent. "How you know that thing ain't the missing link or some such a thing and don't need some studying done on it? Why hell, that thing's liable to be some of these folk's kin folk." The small crowd guffawed, and Hap looked over at Jambo who was creasing and recreasing the two dollar bills Hap had given him.

"He ain't no kin of mine. Is he kin of yours, young fella?" Hap asked the boy.

Jambo glanced up from the money, wide-eyed, and shook his head quickly without committing a yes or no, uncertain of what Hap had said but alert enough to be suspicious.

"You ain't a going blind, is you, young fella?" Hap added.

Jambo looked up and, catching Hap's grin, nodded a decisive no this time.

Headed back to Redbone with the pine box in the truck, Newt counted out the money, giving Jefferson his fifty before dividing the rest of the money equally between them.

"That beats everything I ever seen," Newt said, money in hand. "Them folks sure believed it all right. They were just sure that thing was some kind of alien till that woman hollered 'satan.' But when you think about it, they just seen him like he is right now, all slicked up and shaved. They didn't get a chance to see him before, like we did."

"I seed him a heap of times and it got worser looking every time I throwed that sheet off," Jefferson said.

"What'd all them folks say when they was inside the tent?" Newt asked.

"They asked a heap of questions 'bout where he be from and reckon what he like to eat. But I just folded up my arms, pointed to that badge when they asked me something," Jefferson answered.

"What'd they act like right when you threw the sheet off?" Newt asked.

"Some looked to faint, some moaned. Called to God, some of 'em. Jesus, too."

"What you planning on doing with that chimp now, Mr. Hap? You really planning on getting him a nice casket to bury him in?"

Hap flashed a twinkling eye on the boy. "I figure on taking him over to Ellaville and burying him all right—in that box he's a setting in. I know a sandy, easy to dig in spot where I can lay him to rest. I figure on coming back after a spell and seeing what his bones look like." Hap winked at the boy. "We liable to have us another little tent showing a few years down the road."

"You don't never quit thinking do you, Mr. Hap? What all y'all gonna do with y'all's money anyway?" Newt asked.

"Listen at him." Hap shook his head. "You sure got a knack for asking the right question, young fella. I've had my eye on something for a spell. It's sure got that moneymaking smell to it. I'm figuring you two boys to take an interest in it."

"What you had your eye on?" Newt asked.

"A little land trading, Mr. Newt. I know a man up in Monroe County what done got his self in a little tight. Eighty acres is what he's got, and we can buy it off of him for a hundred and forty dollars. A man could cut him enough timber off that piece of ground to pay for it."

"Dog. We got that much. We could buy it. Me and Jefferson been wanting to buy us some land."

"Well, young fella, I done took a liking to you two, figure we could make us a little team out of it. Ain't exactly no matching pair, but I reckon it'll do." Hap winked again at the boy.

"We'll throw in with you." Newt turned to Jefferson. "Won't we?"

"That too far to go off farming," Jefferson said.

"Farming?" Hap looked over to Jefferson and smiled. "Dirt farming ain't what I got in mind, friend. I wasn't gonna tell y'all at first. Was planning on leaving it for a surprise. But that land joins up to the governor's home place."

"Governor Talmadge?"

"Yes sir. Governor Talmadge."

"Well I'll just be damned," Newt said before he realized he had said it. "We could own some land right next to the governor." He nudged Jefferson with his elbow.

"If a man had him a pocket full of money, he could make his self a fortune buying up land off folks what's got to sell," Hap said.

Newt nudged Jefferson again.

"I'll tell you fine fellas what. Equal partners, same as before."

"You got a deal, Mr. Hap."

Newt nudged Jefferson again. "See there. Our first piece of land and it joins the governor. Papa would of probably already done bought it if he had of known about it."

CHAPTER 19

Early Saturday morning, Jefferson and Newt drove into the clearing of Beaucat's farm. A cold wind from the northwest had blown a thin, cross-stitched blanket of clouds into the Georgia sky. Between the tree line and the clouds, the horizon held a strange aqua tint, as if some distant ocean had overflowed its shelf.

The boy spotted Beaucat first. "There he is, way back there at the barn, waving at us." Jefferson turned the truck and weaved around the side of the house, following behind Beaucat's long but relaxed gait to park behind the barn. Beaucat stopped at the barn door and turned, something between aggravation and speculation in his eyes, a hint of burden in his voice.

"Lord have mercy, child. Y'all done had old Beaucat running hard this morning."

"That whiskey you making just seems to sell itself, Mr. Beaucat," Newt said. "Everybody's always bragging on it, going on and on about how good it is. If this keeps up, we're liable to have to get two stills and two trucks."

Beaucat managed to flash a grin and shake his head. "Listen at him. That one still 'bout to run me ragged. How many cases y'all gone need this morning?"

"Sixteen," Newt said.

Beaucat gave a short nod as if he somehow already knew what the count would be. "I got some of y'all's load in this old barn. Then I'm gone need y'all to come on to the creek, help me haul a load from down there."

Jefferson backed the truck to the door of the barn, where they loaded eleven cases. Then Beaucat threw the saddlebags on the bay mule, and they walked around the front of the house to the trail toward the still. Beaucat led the way, with Jefferson following close behind. Newt rested his hand on the mule's back flank and relaxed into the shuffling rhythm of the mule's hooves drumming toward the rising hiss of the shoals.

A few hundred yards away, Sheriff Wills and Eugene Raintree were following a safe distance behind Earl Ham from the crossroads in Redbone. When Earl drove into the clearing at Beaucat's place, the sheriff pulled off on the edge of the road and turned to Eugene. "You best get on out and walk from here," he said. "I'll go back to where we turned off the main road and meet you there when you get done. You ain't got no gun hid nowhere, do you, son?"

Eugene tongued the tobacco deep into his jowl and popped his mouth open with a moist sound. "Naw sir," Eugene said, patting the front bulge of his overalls. "I been hunting a fore without no gun."

"Sonny wants it done just like he says. We don't want to rile Sonny up now, you hear?"

Eugene, nodding with his dry lip caught on his long front teeth, choked down a rising cackle as he got out of the truck. The sheriff watched Eugene angle off the road toward the wood line. Although in his mid-twenties, Eugene had the appearance of a still-growing boy in his late teens. His arms were disproportionately long to his body, and he swung them with a self-assured cockiness as he walked, neck craned toward the edge of the woods. Wearing the round-topped felt hat common to mountain folks, Eugene kept the top button of his flannel shirt fastened tight at the throat. His large brogan boots, which were unlaced with the pants legs of his overalls tucked into them, seemed oversized even to his sprawling frame. The sheriff watched the red and black flannel disappear into the pine thicket before he turned the truck around and went back to the main road to find a place to pull off and wait.

Earl Ham parked in front of the walnut tree at Beaucat's. The house had a cold, hushed look about it. But he walked up on the porch and knocked on the door anyway, then leaned forward to listen for any footsteps inside. He studied for a moment the tree line of the creek and then sat in the chair on the front porch and lit his cigar, letting the gray smoke drift toward the furrowed clouds. After a few minutes, he let go a sigh, a discontented blow like a mule loaded and looking up a hill. He lifted out of his chair and grunted down the stairs sideways toward the trailhead leading to the still.

Eugene had worked his way around the edge of the clearing on the same wood line that Earl was walking down, ready to jump out and cut him off from the truck if he decided to run. As Earl labored to within a few yards, Eugene slid out from behind the tree, his head cocked slightly back and looking down his nose as if studying the feathers on a young wild turkey to determine whether it was a hen or a jake. "Well looky, by God, here. Just when I thought hunting done gone all to hell this morning, out steps a big 'un."

Earl staggered sideways in an unsteady half step and then regained his composure enough to feel in his back pocket and make sure the gun was there. "Good morning, neighbor," Earl said, moving back two steps and taking off his hat with his left hand, his right hand resting awkwardly on his hip. "Mighty fine morning, ain't it? I don't believe I've had the pleasure. They call me Earl, Earl Ham."

Eugene parted his lips, showing all his long teeth as he spoke the words in an unsettling plainness, as if repeating them slowly enough for someone to write them down. "Pleasure's a mighty

polite word, ain't it, mister? I know who you is. You the man I
been setting here a waiting on."

"Say I am?" Earl squinted over Eugene's back as if trying to
distinguish the shade of his words, the color of their discontent.
"Well I'll sure be glad to help you out if I can. What you hunting
this morning, neighbor?"

"One cocksucker's all. Been on a cold trail till now."

"One cock...?" Earl started to repeat the phrase as if perhaps
it was an unfamiliar game bird, but caught himself as its meaning
became clear. He mustered a nervous smile out of a down-turned
mouth. "I sure wouldn't want to get off on the wrong foot with a
new friend, neighbor. They's some folks 'round here that say they
ain't no problem that's too big for Earl Ham to work out, and
friend, if we got us a problem, I'm sure we can work out
something where all parties will feel like they been took care of."

"Well, Sadie twist her petticoat." The hillbilly spit brown and
sped up the rhythm of his speech. "That's some mighty fancy
words, some real pretty talking you just done. But I ain't got no
say so in it, mister. Same way a double ax blade don't got no say in
where it's a going, just follows where the handle aims it. The
thing is, mister, I ain't in the dealing business. I'm more in what
you might call learning folks the error of they ways business. And
you're double due a little learning is what I been a hearing. Fact is,
them folks up the river done got a whiff of that panther piss you
been spreading up there, and, well sir, it's done got to stinking to
'em."

Earl glanced briefly at the sky and then bowed his head
slightly to invoke some reverence into his words. "Neighbor, and I
hope you don't mind me calling you that, neighbor, 'cause I
believe like the good book says that you ought to love your
neighbor, and that's what I aim to do. And, neighbor, now that
you've helped me see the error of my ways, I'd like to propose an

offering of cash money that I believe you'll be most satisfied with."

Eugene gave a mocking glance toward the sky as if to make sure Earl had not seen something there. "Them Bible words don't sound near as pretty coming out your mouth as them fancy ones did." Eugene then moved nose to nose with Earl and rolled his shoulders. "Ever hear of this 'un, neighbor—'if thy tongue offends thee, pluck it on out'?"

Earl, who had been holding his mouth slightly parted like an old man who had long since quit using his nose to breathe, quickly closed it. His lips had become white and chalky, making his words thick when he spoke. "I'm sure starting to see what you mean, friend. If you'll allow me to reach in my pocket and see what cash money I got on me, I feel sure I can even up this here deal where everybody'll be..." As Earl twisted to reach into his pocket, Eugene planted his leg behind Earl's knee and slammed him to the ground with his forearm: "Watch your step now, Mr. Preacher Man." Earl fell hard on his side and rolled over to his stomach where he lay still. The hillbilly reached in the front of his overalls and brought out a short black horse whip, twirling it around like a black snake slithering. Eugene took a few steps back and with a long and well-grooved motion cracked the whip over the now-tucked head. Earl lifted himself a few inches off the ground and crept toward the wood line on his hands and knees while Eugene, squalling a hillbilly yodel as if to call his hunting party to a bayed hog, lashed him across the back and thighs. Earl grunted with every blow as he pulled himself along like a leg-shot varmint headed toward cover, his head tucked low between his arms. Eugene put his foot on the seat of Earl's pants and pushed him flat on the ground, feeling the hard pistol in the back pocket as his heel released the shove. Earl rolled over, reaching for the gun. Eugene ran toward him as he saw the weapon rise from the dust and jumped down on Earl. His hip struck Earl's chest at the instant of the gunshot, making it seem as if the force of his weight alone had caused the sound. Eugene squeezed the gun out of Earl's hand and stood over him.

"Well, looky here, Mr. Preacher Man. You doing a little hunting your own self this morning, aint you? Here you was a quoting all them pretty Bible verse words and all the time you just been wanting to play rough."

Eugene tilted his head back and cackled freely, then paced around Earl, stopping to point the gun at his head in different positions as he circled him. "Why didn't you just, by God, tell me you was wanting to play rough from the get go and we could of just gone on and locked up like a couple of boar hogs in a cane thicket? Your name's Ham, ain't it? Bet you could squeal just like an old Hampshire sow if somebody was to ask you real nice. Squeal real pretty like too, I'm a thinking. I just wished I had time to ask you real polite like, but I ain't. I got to go to learning somebody something."

Earl looked up, his hand shielding the glare of the man's face against the sky. Eugene turned the pistol where the butt laid flat in the palm of his hand and, reaching into the air, swung it toward Earl like he was going to hit him, stomping his foot on the ground to fake the sound of impact.

Earl buried his head beneath his arms, and Eugene cocked his head back and squalled again, this time patting his hand on his mouth to add a haunting cadence to the call. Earl peeked out of his arms at the sound, and Eugene slapped Earl behind the ear with the flat butt of the pistol.

Earl crumpled facedown to the ground and did not move. "Get your ass back down to grubbing them worms, sowbelly," Eugene said. "We ain't even got to the two plus twos yet." Then Eugene dug the heel of his brogan into Earl's shoulder and rolled him over, but Earl's body again settled to complete stillness. "You ain't paying good attention, Mr. Preacher Man. How you reckon you gone learn to cipher if you ain't paying attention? I got a little subtracting lesson I'm fixing to learn you."

Newt and Jefferson were halfway to the still when they heard the shot. They left Beaucat holding the mule and moved quickly toward the clearing, stopping as they reached the edge of the wood line. Eugene was standing over Earl, moving the gun in short loose circles around his bloody head. "Now I wouldn't a had to do all that if you hadn't a wanted to play so rough. I reckon you was wanting to get all your lesson at once, mister fancy-talking preacher man."

Jefferson took the burlap bag from the boy without taking his eyes off Eugene. He untied the knot and slid the pistol out as quietly as he could. As he brought the gun up to point it through the bushes, the barrel brushed against the leaves. Eugene turned and walked toward the sound with the gun out in front of him. "Who the hell is that? Who's in yonder rustling?" Jefferson remained steady, holding the gun on Eugene's chest as he moved toward them with his mouth forced closed, stalking the noise.

Afraid that he would be seen if Eugene got any closer, Newt placed his right foot where the exposed root of the tree met the trunk and in one quick motion turned his body sideways to get behind the tree. A twig snapped under his movement. Eugene reached out and fired into the sound.

Jefferson did not hear the sound of his own gun firing. He sensed only a strange disorder of time and motion as the man seemed to hesitate forward before falling backwards, arms flailing at some unforgiving wind, and only then did time reorder itself as the sound of the first shot echoed into the second, settling to the slow smoke of the pistol he now held with a vise-like grip.

Newt fell back against the tree and slid to his haunches. Jefferson turned to the boy's movement and for a moment recognized something of Addie in the boy's face, the jaw not set, the uncomprehending eyes searching to find some object to focus on. But the sharpness quickly returned to Newt's eyes and the urgency in his voice overrode the tremor. "We got to think quick. They'll give you the chair for shooting a white man. Some of 'em'll want to hang you even before the trial. They'll try to say you killed Papa, too. But if we just leave, folks'll think they shot each other. That's what it'll look like to the first person that happens up on 'em. Nobody's here to say different. There ain't nothing we can do for either one of 'em now."

Newt moved into the clearing and gently lifted the pistol out of the grass. He bent down over Earl and studied the familiar body for a long while as if recognizing in it something he had never seen before. "I never seen a dead man this close up before. I'd always imagined 'em to look a little more peaceful. I wonder if it takes long for the soul to get wherever it's going." He squatted beside the body, touching his fingers delicately on his papa's chest. "You reckon it's gone by now?"

Jefferson did not answer. He was crouched by the deputy looking like a man checking a buck he has just shot to make sure it is dead, to see where the bullet landed. Jefferson rolled Eugene's shoulder over to look at his back. "Bullet done gone clean through this 'un."

Newt placed the gun by his papa's hand and stood up straight, studying the aqua horizon in the distance for a long moment as if its strange and surreal tint was some warning, a sign that he had failed to acknowledge. He closed his eyes and concentrated on the montage of flashing images, the short snatches of faces and places that reeled through his mind the same way he had imagined images would come to a dying man. He wondered if perhaps this was the way judgment was delivered—a relentless circling of images that would be replayed in the mind over and over like the never-ending spooning of bad-tasting medicine to the sick. But he found that his mind had settled on one image that doubtless it had been groping for—his father kneeling beside the freshly dug grave.

The boy walked over to Jefferson and squatted beside him. "Them two guns are just alike, the one next to Papa and the one we've got. They're a matching pair of Smith and Wesson 38's that Papa bought off a man from Hillsboro." They studied Eugene's limp body with the flannel shirt open and the white chest red-splotched, looking into the eyes that somehow still managed to hold the same gawk of disbelief.

"I ain't never seed this 'un before," Jefferson said. "Reckon who he is?"

Newt and Jefferson both heard the rattle of the axle and the dead thump of rubber pounding the rutted road before they saw the truck itself. They backed deeper and deeper into the woods as the truck approached, finally lying down in a shallow ravine. Jefferson recognized Sheriff Wills as he stepped out of the truck and walked to stand over Eugene's body, nudging the dead man's shoulder with the toe of his boot. "What in the goddamn hell...."

Newt reached his hand around Jefferson's arm and squeezed it. Then he brought his finger up to his eye and pointed toward Earl's body. It was the elbow they saw move first. The moan was feeble as Earl's hand moved toward the blood above his ear. The body twisted slowly, Earl squinting upward to find the sheriff's eyes upon him.

"Morning, Mr. Earl." The sheriff, sardonic and humorless, unsnapped the leather strap on his pistol. "Looks like hunting's pretty good 'round here. Done got yourself a law man I see."

Earl rolled over to his knees, stood up one leg at a time. He glanced down at his hat on the ground a few feet from him but did not bend to pick it up. The long pieces of hair that he usually kept combed from one side to the other to cover his bald spot stuck out from the left side of his head like the brow tine of a deer's antler.

"Done got what?" Earl asked. "What happened?"

"Why hell, Earl, let's see if we can't figure this here out. We got us a gun laying by your hand, my deputy sheriff laying on the ground shot in the chest, dead as a hammer. By God, it appears we got us a killing on our hands, don't it?"

"He's dead?" Earl Ham asked.

The sheriff glanced over the body. "I don't speck even your money'll get that 'un breathing again."

"He just come out of nowhere, Sheriff, knocked me out cold from behind," Earl said.

"Uh-huh," the sheriff said, chin cradled in his hand. Then he pointed at the body in the grass. "That 'un there knocked you out cold, did he?"

"Yes sir, Sheriff. I'll put my hand on the Bible," Earl said, raising his hand almost to his shoulder.

"Well sir, that don't leave but one question then. Did you shoot him *before* or *after* he knocked you out?"

Earl's eyes darted toward the body in confusion. "Why hell. Neither one of 'em. I couldn't a shot him. That's what I'm telling you. I was out cold."

The sheriff reached down, picked up the gun by the barrel, and walked over to Earl, holding the gun in front of his face. "This your gun?"

"Yes sir, but—"

"Mr. Earl. This here man laying at your feet is my deputy. Meet Mr. Eugene Raintree. Mr. Earl. I'm hoping you'll excuse the late introductions. He was following a lead on moonshine whiskey what was coming cross county lines from down here."

The sheriff came nose to nose with Earl much like Eugene had done earlier. "Now you in the moonshine whiskey business if I ain't mistaken, ain't you? And this here 38 is your pistol, ain't it? And that there is a dead deputy sheriff laying over yonder, ain't it?" The sheriff surveyed the field around him, settling his eyes on two black objects at the end of the field. "Or maybe you saying one of them two crows landed on top of that Smith and Wesson and pecked the trigger off?"

"I couldn't a shot nobody, Sheriff. I was out cold."

"Mr. Earl Ham. You got the right to remain silent. Anything that you say can and will be used against you in a court of law. Now, get over here and help me load this man you done killed into the front seat of this truck."

Earl reached down and grabbed Eugene's feet, and the sheriff grabbed Eugene's arms under his shoulders, working his way backwards until he had the body in the front seat of the truck. "Now get in there and hold him up where he won't fall over," the sheriff said. "We all going to the jailhouse."

CHAPTER 20

The next Wednesday morning at Mr. Bludie's store, a crowd gathered around the potbellied stove behind the meat counter. Three farmers who sharecropped Earl's cotton, Raspus and Frenchy McCall and Buck Jackson, backed up against the stove while Mr. Bludie cut up whole chickens into frying parts over a deep-rutted butcher block. One old-timer leaned back in a chair against the side wall.

"Yes sir," Mr. Bludie said. "Looks like old Earl done high-stepped his self into a bad row a stumps this time."

"I ain't for sure he can back his plow out of this 'un," Buck said.

The old man got up from his chair, bent over, and spit a quick stream of tobacco juice into the sand beneath the potbellied stove. "That man was weeding one hell of a wide row for a spell though."

"Godalmighty what you talking 'bout," Buck said. "That man had a plenty of money."

"Shit. That man done made enough money to set fire to a wet mule if he had a mind to," Raspus said.

"Reckon he'll do any time?" Mr. Bludie looked up from the chicken and over his glasses to the old man who had spit.

"I reckon he could," Raspus said. "You know what they say. Old big coon walks late. But the right dog'll put that ass up a tree."

"Aw hell," the old man grumbled. "A hip full of money'll take down the law any day."

"I don't know," Mr. Bludie said. "They saying Sheriff Wills has got Earl dead to rights this time. They got Earl's pistol. The sheriff knew the boy's mama, too. What was his name?"

"Raintree."

"That's it, Eugene, ain't it? Yeah. They say Sheriff Wills is hell-bound to get old Ham this time."

"We'll see," the old-timer said.

"Who's the judge?"

"Judge Long, they claim."

"Whoa, Lord. Look out now. Him and Sonny goes way back."

"I know one thing. That man don't play. He'd as soon put your skinny ass on the chain gang as look at you."

"Shit," Buck said. "I don't never want to be standing in front of that man when he's waving that little hammer in his hand."

"They say old Earl's tight with the governor, got that autograph picture of him and all," Raspus said. "Reckon old Gene'll come down here and bail him out the jailhouse?"

"Old Gene? Hell naw. Old Gene's too busy keeping his own ass out of trouble to be worrying with a Ham hock," Buck said, using his pocket knife to slice off a plug of tobacco.

"I tell you one by-god thing, old Gene could damn sure handle it if he wanted to," Raspus said.

"Damned if that ain't a fact," Buck said.

"Who's Earl got for his lawyer?"

"That Upchurch fella from Atlanta," Mr. Bludie said.

"Good godalmighty damn. That'll set him back."

"They claim he's the best."

"Got him a silver tongue's what they claim."

"They say that man could talk the britches right off a queen," Buck said.

"She'd be too old for me," Frenchy said, shaking his head.

"I didn't say he was gonna hump it. I just said he *could* if he wanted to," Buck said.

"Good godalmighty."

"How old is the queen anyway?" Frenchy asked.

"Aw hell."

"Who's running the mill now?" Buck asked.

"They say Newt's been up at the mill," Mr. Bludie said. "Ain't been to school since the killing, they claim."

"I'll be damned," Buck said. "I reckon that boy probably could run that mill if he's to set his mind to it."

"That boy there's got a head on him, now."

"Plenty smart, that young 'un."

"They say he takes after his mama."

"He do look like her."

"Don't look none like his papa, that's a fact."

"We liable to be on halves with that boy 'fore it's all over with," Buck said.

"Be all right with me long as his papa don't come out in him," Raspus said.

"You reckon any of the rest of his children'll be at the trial?" Frenchy asked.

"Who's?"

"Old Earl's."

"You mean Addie?"

"Naw hell." Frenchy flung his hand in an expansive gesture. "All the rest of them babies he done seeded in across these hills."

"Some folks say he got more colored babies than white 'uns," Raspus said.

"That's a heap a little brown Earls running 'round."

"Liable to be a few Earlenes throwed in there, too."

"Lord have mercy."

"Old Earl's sashaying days is over, I speck."

"What you talking 'bout. His stumping days is through, boy."

"They set bail?"

"Ain't no bail," Mr. Bludie said. "He'll be there till trial."

"How's Miss Naomi taking it?"

"She all right, they say," Mr. Bludie said.

"I'm surprised she ain't done hightailed it on back to South Carolina," Frenchy said.

"Might be waiting 'round to see how the money gonna shake out," Buck said.

"Why hell, I know I would be. Ain't no way I'd stay with that big-ass bastard all them years and then pick up and leave on pay day," Frenchy said.

"I'm surprised she ain't done been gone, what with Earl sticking his old nose up every skirt on every hog trail and dirt road in the county," Raspus said.

"Gingham sacks's more like it."

"Don't reckon she give a damn what he was sniffing up under long as it wasn't up hers," Buck said.

"Godalmighty damn."

"Surely that fella from Argentina'll show back up to character witness for old Earl," Buck said, rolling the tobacco plug from one side of his jaw to the other.

"Anybody ever find him?"

"Not that I know of," said Mr. Bludie. "His folks come 'round here looking for him after he didn't show up back home. Had the sheriff with 'em. The sheriff said they could talk some English, but I'll be damned if I could understand what they was saying. His wife, she just kept holding out some big old silver coins in the palm of her hand and pointing to 'em. I'm thinking that man was up here to buy him some land. A right smart of land if I ain't mistaken."

"Big old silver dollars, you say?" Buck asked.

CHAPTER 21

As Newt walked behind the deputy, the long corridor seemed to broaden with the sounds of hard leather striking the concrete floor. The deputy opened the cell door where Earl Ham sat on an iron cot with his sock feet on the floor and hands folded in his lap, raising his head only when the door clanked firmly shut. Newt walked past his father and squatted in the corner the way a carpenter's helper sits, stealing precious seconds off an unforgiving clock.

Earl placed his hands on his knees and leaned forward, riveting his steel blue eyes on the boy. The springs beneath the mattress groaned into his first words. "I didn't kill that deputy, son."

"I know that, Papa." Newt's voice was quiet, soothing.

"I've been thinking, son. When I get out of here, me and you, we'll spend some time together. The first thing I'm gone do is send that brother of yours off someplace where they can take care of his kind. Without him around, we'll have more time to spend together. Why hell, we can even go to church now and then if that's what you want. I'll teach you everything you need to know 'bout being a man. How'd you like that, boy?"

Newt listened obligingly to the rare tone of regret in the words, and he recognized in his father's eyes something that he had never seen in them before, a brief yet unmistakable vulnerability, a longing much like his brother's eyes held when he lost his grip on a slick turtle's back and watched it scoot back in the water. Though this was unsettling to the boy, it could not deter the question that he had prepared to ask.

"You remember that man from Argentina, Papa?"

Earl's eyes locked on the boy like a snake drawing its venom from within, but Newt remained unflinching. The boy waited patiently for the sound and meaning of his words to be complete, fulfilled, the way the sound of a bell settles silently into one's own self.

"I was up that morning way before everybody else. I was at the kitchen window when your headlights come down the road. It was way before sunup. But you drove out across the pasture toward the bottom instead of coming up to the house. I tore out across that pasture"—Newt lifted his eyes into his father's—"to see if you would take me fishing. I was eight, and I remember it being a Saturday. By the time I got there you were digging a hole hard and fast. I could tell something wasn't right. So I just kept hid in the bushes until you opened the trunk of your car and drug that body out. I stayed right there, hardly even breathing, until you covered that man with dirt and smoothed it out. Then you took two trunks out of your car and I watched you bury them, too. Both of 'em. All these years, I haven't breathed a word of it to a soul. You're the first one I told."

Earl's lip curled. His beady pupils penetrated into the boy's eyes, probing toward the inception of the words themselves as if the burning in his eyes alone could curdle their meaning. Earl stood and moved to the cell door with more quickness than his size belied. He looked down the hall both ways and then came back to stand over the boy, the gruffness back in his voice. "What in the hell are you saying, boy? Huh? You think you got something on me? I tell you what you got. You ain't got shit. You think you know something about who I am? I'll tell you, by God, who I am. I'm Earl Ham, the man who ain't let nothing stand in the way of getting what the fuck he wants, and if you think I'm stopping now, then you got shit for brains, boy. I got one idea you might not a thought of yet. How 'bout I just whip your smart-talking ass right here in this jail cell?"

Newt stood up in front of his father, like a young soldier erect toward the horizon of battle. "You could whip me, Papa. But that won't change anything. I been studying it for a long time, all the different ways you made Mama and Addie suffer. I always thought that it was like God was testing us somehow, that if we just took enough of it we'd pass the test and things would get all right again. But I lost hope on that and then started hoping that one day you'd see it and change. But that didn't happen either. So I had to make a choice. I dug up those boxes of silver and moved 'em to where nobody knows where they are but me. If something was to ever happen to me, that silver'll be gone forever.

"I came here to make a deal with you, Papa." Newt went to the cot and sat down where his father had sat. The boy was silent for several seconds, wringing his hands before he spoke again. "I believe I know a way to get you out of here. If you're figuring on walking out of this place one day, then you need to listen real careful to what I've got to say. I'm bringing all the deeds to the land and the mill in here, and you're gonna sign 'em over to Mama. Then you'll leave Redbone and go back to where you came from. When they do let you out, the first thing you'll do is come by the house and take Addie in your arms and you're gonna hold him and tell him you love him. He might not understand all the words you're saying, but he'll know what you mean just by holding him. Then you're gonna turn to Mama and tell her that everything that went wrong between y'all is all your fault and none of hers, that you're leaving 'cause it's the only right thing left to do. That's when I'll tell you where them boxes of silver are hid and you can get 'em and be gone. I figure that'll be enough to get you started again."

Earl had stopped looking at Newt as he spoke. He winced into the pale light coming in the window as if the words themselves were not spoken by the boy but permeated the cell like the stench of a dead animal uncovered by absolute chance, a stray foot in soft ground. Earl blew as if exhaling a long-held stale wind. He quickly turned on the boy. Twisting a handful of Newt's shirt below his throat with his left hand, his father raised him off the cot and pulled his hair tight with his right hand from behind. He slowly brought the boy's eyes into his own. "Suffering?" Earl spit over the boy's shoulder, then glared back into his eyes. "You don't know shit about suffering, boy. You don't know a goddamned thing about being a man, 'bout making something out of nothing. Don't flesh and blood mean nothing to you, boy? Don't that mean a goddamned thing to you?" Earl released the boy, slinging him back against the wall.

Newt gathered himself at the wall and stood straight again. "That's the only thing that does make it hard, Papa."

"What if I just say hell no, boy? No deal. You just gonna let your own flesh and blood rot in this cell?"

"Then I reckon it'll be left up to the court to say what needs to be done."

"Well goddamn. While you reckoning, boy, suppose you tell me why in the hell I ought to reckon the same little piss-ant that don't hold flesh and blood no count can get me out of here?"

"You'll just have to believe I can, Papa."

"Believe? Believe what? That I ought to just up and leave everything I done built, everything I done worked my whole life for?"

"Except for that silver."

"What if I was to say I'd make it up to you and your mama, boy?"

"I thought about that. You could've, Papa, a long time ago. But that time's past. You can't no more, even if you wanted to."

"But your little piss-ant ass can?"

"No sir. I can't change nothing that's already happened. But if I don't try and take away what I know is killing 'em, eating the very life out of 'em, then I won't be able to live with myself no more. I done looked at it every way I can, Papa. I know I might not be all that much. But they ain't got nobody but me. I ain't really figured out yet why I was the one called on to do it. I reckon I just was."

Earl walked over to the cell door. "Hey, deputy. Get this boy out of here."

Newt did not look at his papa's face as he walked through the cell door. He walked through the jail and out of the hall without speaking to anyone, without hearing his own footsteps or those of the deputy's. He came out into the autumn morning without seeing the cool breeze shake the yellow poplar leaves or even the mule quarter-turned and staring at him as he walked toward the truck. He got in the passenger side and turned to Jefferson. "We got to go to Hillsboro."

Even though Jefferson sensed that his destiny, the very question of his freedom, depended on what had taken place in the jail cell that morning, he asked nothing of the boy, allowing him to ride in silence all the way to the crossroads in Hillsboro. When Newt finally spoke, he did not turn his head from looking out the window across the fields. The morning sun already held a distance to it, and he watched the long horizon gather itself against the pine ridges. "I heard Mama say it once, a long time ago. She was talking to my aunt. But she didn't know I heard it. Said she had only ever loved one man. It wasn't Papa either. I could tell by the way she said it."

At the store, Newt turned the knob and cracked the door open. McAllister was sitting at his desk. He was startled but quickly managed a broad and sincere smile. "Newt boy," he said, taking his glasses off his nose and laying them on top of the opened book. "I didn't expect to see you so soon."

Newt sat down in the chair in front of McAllister's desk. "I'll get right to the point, Mr. McAllister. Folks say you're a lawyer."

"I have practiced law," McAllister said.

"I need for you to answer a question for me."

"I'll do the best I can, son."

"Can a judge decide a murder case by his self in a jury trial, or will it all be left up to the jury by the time it gets that far?"

McAllister moved to the back of his chair and studied the boy as if he saw something different in his eyes. They possessed a familiarity that McAllister seemed to struggle to place, the way a thought, at once urgent and magnificent, somehow escapes the plowed furrow of the mind.

McAllister leaned forward. "I'm sorry about your papa, Newt. I know it's got to be hard on all of you. How's your mama taking it?"

"She ain't really said all that much."

McAllister relaxed back in his chair, waiting a moment to make sure the boy had said all he had wanted to say. "Well, in almost all murder trials, the jury does decide the fate of the accused. But there have been some cases which the judge decides." McAllister put on his glasses, then walked to a set of books hardbound in red and silver and fingered slowly through them, finally pulling one off the shelf. He opened the book and started reading. "Ah, yes. Here it is. If a lawyer asks for a directed verdict of acquittal, then the judge does have the option to decide the verdict himself."

"You mean, if he wanted to, a judge could decide a defendant is not guilty without the jury having nothing to say about it?" Newt asked.

"That's right. The judge could then dismiss the case before the jury has even deliberated over the verdict."

"Has it happened before?"

"I've never personally seen it happen, but, yes, it has."

"Can the judge just decide to do it on his own?"

"Well, the defense attorney would have to request it."

"So the lawyer just asks for it and then the judge decides to do it or not do it?"

McAllister nodded.

"What exactly does the lawyer ask for?"

"He makes a motion for a directed verdict of acquittal."

"But if the lawyer asks for it, and the judge decides to dismiss the case, then it's done?"

"That's right."

Newt's arms were out in front of him on the desk. His thin arms were folded, and, with his grandfather's frayed felt fedora on his slightly bowed head, he looked like a patient old man at ease with the annoyance of moments passing. After two or three minutes, his green eyes lightly sparkled beneath the shadowed brim as he lifted his eyes to McAllister. "I got just one more favor I need to ask of you."

McAllister leaned forward. "I'll do what I can."

"I need for somebody to draw up some deeds," he said, moving to the end of his seat. "Saying my papa's giving everything he owns to my mama. Are you able to do that sort of thing?"

McAllister nodded.

"Would you do that for me?"

"Yes."

The boy closed his eyes briefly, then rose out of his chair and moved behind McAllister's desk, extending his hand. "I can't say exactly how I knew it. I just had this feeling. The very first time me and Jefferson met you down at the ferry, I could tell you was the kind of man that would help somebody if they really needed helping. I'll make it up to you somehow. I ain't sure how, but I will."

CHAPTER 22

On Friday, the third day of the trial, Sheriff Wills was scheduled to testify. The sawmills in Berner and Redbone had not been running since the trial began, and early every morning the trucks and wagons gathered around the town square and overflowed into the side streets and alleyways. Since the trial occupied most of the sheriff's time, the town had quickly assumed a reckless and free spirit, fueled in part by the brisk November air. Chickens and dogs were traded off the town square, and whiskey was drunk from tin cups in the open. At night most of the wagons camped at Tarentine's Ferry. The fiddle music lingered deep into the night as fighting cocks spurred and bled in the light of campfires, their pirouetting shadows dancing out into the woods.

The trial was held on the second floor of the antebellum courthouse building. The courtroom with its high ceilings and oak floors was packed with folks from both Redbone and Berner. The black sharecroppers and their women crowded into the balcony and sat in sullen bemusement at the spit-shined exchanges of the attorneys. Most of the crowd had something at stake, a lost job at the Redbone mill, a sharecropping deal with Earl Ham, or a loan for a mule or plow that could be washed clean with the verdict.

Newt sat on the second row behind his father and Mr. Upchurch. He listened intently to the proceedings, but mostly he tracked the faces of the judge and the jurors, sizing up every twitch and expression as they reacted to the testimony.

Judge Long was in his early fifties. His dark bushy eyebrows contrasted sharply with his graying temples and pale full jowls. The judge had a reputation for stiff sentences and no foolishness, glaring to silence any noise in the courtroom that he judged too loud or unnecessary. Newt had caught the judge staring at him twice while Upchurch stood and spoke from the defense table. Each time Newt had maneuvered past the stare by turning and focusing on the witnesses.

The prosecutor was a young but aggressive attorney named Horace Whatley. He had a reputation for having the tenacity and quickness of a rat terrier, and his small wiry frame did seem to move more by reflex than calculation. The large round glasses worn tight against his eyes gave him a brief air of distinction that was quickly dispelled by the short-cropped tuft of dark hair that fell directly above his forehead like a rooster's comb. Using what appeared to be all the muscles in his neck and upper body, Whatley could muster only a high cracked whine when he spoke, similar to a juvenile rooster coaxing the sunrise.

At midmorning of the third day, Whatley called Sheriff Wills to the stand. Without the black gun belt and holster around his waist, the sheriff looked to Newt only partially dressed, a sharecropper without his hat or a blacksmith without his hammer and apron. The sheriff took his seat after the bailiff swore him in and shifted his knees slightly and awkwardly toward the jury.

"State your name please."

"Sheriff Wills."

"State your full name for the record please, Sheriff."

The sheriff shifted in his seat. "Theophilis P. Wills." High-pitched cackles were released through the crowd, fading out in the balcony as the sheriff's face turned red, and Judge Long arched his bushy eyebrows across the room.

"State your occupation, please."

"Sheriff of Butts County, Georgia."

"How long have you served in that capacity, sir, as sheriff of Butts County, Georgia?" Whatley asked.

"Sixteen years."

"Sheriff, can you tell the jury what you saw on the morning of November 3, 1937?"

"Well, sir, me and my deputy, Eugene Raintree, drove down the river road toward Redbone to do some investigating as to the source of some illegal moonshine whiskey activity crossing over the line here into Butts County. Fact is, we heard it was coming from down around Sweetwater Branch. So we decided to drive on down to the suspected location. I dropped Eugene off at the clearing so he could nose around and get us a lead that would help us make a case."

"So Sheriff, you were on an official criminal investigation on the day of November 3. Just doing sheriff business?"

"Yes sir."

"So you dropped Deputy Raintree off. Then what did you do?"

"I parked the truck up the road and out of sight while Eugene went in there to see what he could find."

"How long were you parked in your truck at that location, Sheriff?"

"I'd say thirty to thirty-five minutes."

"Did you see any other cars coming or going while you were parked at that location?"

"No sir."

"And what made you leave that location after thirty to thirty-five minutes, Sheriff?"

"I heard a gunshot."

"You heard a gunshot?"

"Yes sir."

"One gunshot?"

"Yes sir. One gunshot."

"Are you positive it couldn't have been two gunshots, maybe fired real close together?" Whatley asked.

"Yes sir. I'm sure. I waited another minute or two to see if I heard another one after the first one. But there wasn't no other shot."

"What did you do then, Sheriff?"

"I turned the car around and hightailed it down to where I heard that gunshot go off at."

"How long did it take you to get to where you heard that one gunshot, Sheriff?"

"'Bout five minutes, I'd say."

"Can you tell the jury what you saw when you got there?"

"Yes sir. My deputy, Eugene, was on the ground laying face up and shot in the chest. Earl Ham was setting on the ground with a Smith and Wesson 38 pistol laying right beside him."

"Sheriff, is that man—the man you saw sitting on the ground with the pistol by his side and your deputy Raintree lying a few feet away, shot in the chest—is that man in this courtroom today?"

"Yes sir."

"Can you point him out to us?"

"Yes sir." The sheriff kept his elbow close to his stomach while raising his hand in front of his face, pointing his forefinger toward Earl seated at the table. "That's him, setting right there."

Whatley walked around to Earl's side of the table without taking his eyes off the sheriff. He gestured toward Earl with a flowing open palm. "This man?" he asked.

"Yes sir."

"I have no further questions, Your Honor."

"Does the defense wish to cross-examine?" Judge Long asked.

"Yes, your honor."

Upchurch rose from the defense table, wearing a gray tweed suit with black suspenders and a red tie. Not so much handsome

"I'd like to tell you. But I already decided that if I didn't tell you why we was going then you couldn't ever be accused of doing something wrong if you didn't know what it was you was doing. And I'll back you up, that you didn't know nothing, if it comes to it. Then if nothing goes wrong while I'm there, I'll tell you on the way back."

Jefferson longed to hear some final words from the boy, the pure and reconciled certainty of his fate as only the boy could tell it. But he was afraid even to speak the words, as if by asking the question, the answer itself might escape as an echo escapes a hollow, settling upon distant, uncaring ears. He had not even dared tell Ida. He had simply and silently hoped to be forgiven without so much as muttering a prayer for it, fearing that the prayer, the formal request itself, might somehow entangle the delicate weave that protected him.

"How long do it take to die in that chair?" Jefferson asked.

"I ain't real sure, but I wouldn't think it'd take too awful long," Newt said.

"Do it make any kind a noise when they cuts it on you?" Jefferson asked.

Newt turned toward Jefferson, studying his eyes carefully before he spoke again. "It ain't nothing to worry about. They say it makes a sizzling sound at first, but it'd probably knock you out right off where you can't hear it or feel nothing neither."

Jefferson slowed the truck as they passed the small church and graveyard on the edge of town. He pulled off the road and stopped when he saw the first hazy glimmer of light from Jula Mae's house through the trees.

"I'll get on out here and you pull this truck around that church lot we just passed. Have it turned toward Redbone and just wait for me. I don't reckon I'll be too long."

Newt climbed out of the truck and walked down the road, keeping his eyes on the yellow light gently pulsing from the back window of the house. He crouched down low when he spotted the black Ford reflecting the back porch light. It was parked behind the shed, not fully hidden from the road. *I sure hope she ain't got no bad dogs,* he thought, reaching into his coat pocket to feel of the biscuits and bacon he had brought to feed them if it came to it. Squatting quietly, he slowed his breath to where he could not even hear it himself, listening for the movement of dogs under the house or tied near the back steps. He moved as if he were still hunting by the creek, picking his way from bare spot to bare spot on the ground so his feet would not crunch the leaves. Stopping below the window of the room where the light was shining brightest, he strained to hear the low muffled voices through the walls. He could only see the ceiling, the one yellow bulb and the beaded pine boards from where he stood.

He climbed the first strong limb of an elm at the back corner of the house and stood up, holding his hand against the trunk of the tree for balance. He rose to see a man and woman already there, in full view at the foot of the quilted bed, his pale silver neck and loose-skinned chest against her graceful black hands, working across the stiff body. Her long back, muscled and narrow at the waist, was purplish in the yellow light as she slithered down the chest to his white thighs and there bobbed in a slow inevitable rhythm. It was the long and bushy dark eyebrows that the boy first recognized. The judge's head was cocked back toward the ceiling. He looked to be working his gums, smacking his lips together like an old man with his false teeth out, trying to moisten his mouth. He stood with his hands by his side, his thighs slightly spread. His pose was that of baptizing, riverbank reverence, a man praying, turning toward the heavens with his eyes closed, the bare feet inching along the muddy bank toward the balance of immersion.

She rose up and kissed him on the mouth, pulling him down out of Newt's sight.

Newt climbed out of the tree and sat on the ground. With a stub of a pencil, he printed carefully on a brown paper bag he had brought: "WANTED TO HAVE A WORD WITH YOU BUT SEEN YOU WAS BUSY." He worked his way around the edge of the woods behind the shed and to the black car, placing the note under the windshield wiper. At first he thought it was the movement of the windshield wiper that made the faint groan, but the sound became a slow growl that spread across the ground like a damp fog. He turned carefully and saw only the yellow eyes and the pointed black ears, the flash of red tongue between the click and snarl of teeth. He ran before he remembered the bacon and biscuits in his pocket. He ran away from the light and into the bushes like a halfback, the arms of young saplings slapping against his face and shoulders until he felt the heat of the dog's mouth at his backside, like the warmth of a saw motor itself as it revs and idles, setting the teeth in one direction. It was not the wide-mouthed bite that he had anticipated, but the sharp sting of the teeth nipping his thigh as he ran. He jumped to the first limb of a young cedar tree, not knowing that it was a cedar or that it was even a tree, just feeling its size near him the way a drowning man flails above the water for a rope or stick. He scaled the tree and felt his thigh. The pants leg was opened and wet, and he heard the woman's voice from the back door shouting, "Who that? What you done treed, dog?" He heard the screen door slam as the dog bayed vapor at his feet, leaping against the trunk of the cedar and twisting back to the ground. Newt did not know whether the slamming of the door meant that he or she or both were coming out into the darkness toward him. He threw the first piece of bacon at the dog's feet and the thick bristled neck followed the falling motion, eating it a few inches off the ground as if it had bounced into his mouth.

Newt snatched off a cedar limb above his head and threw the remaining pieces of bacon and biscuit over the dog and toward the house. The dog growled at the movement of his arm as he threw and then disappeared back into the bushes after the food. Newt hit the ground and ran with the cedar bough in his hand until he got to the clearing of the graveyard at the church, not knowing whether the heat that ran with him was of the dog or himself, his own blood hot, rising from his thigh. He turned and raised the limb against the woods and waited for the dog, straining through his own panting to listen into the silence. He ran to the truck and jumped in. "Roll up your window and head this thing on to Redbone. That's one bad dog. I'd still be in that cedar tree if I hadn't a brought along that bacon."

"Dog?" Jefferson repeated. "He get you?"

Newt felt underneath his thigh and put his hand into the light on the windshield. "It's bleeding some, but it don't seem all that bad."

Jefferson took off the bandana from his neck and handed it to Newt. "Tie this here up around it to help stop the bleeding."

"Doggone, Jefferson. That was too close there. I was sure hoping she wouldn't a had no bad dogs. That thing looked like a old black wolf. I reckon it was worth it, though. I had to see for myself. I couldn't take nobody's word for that. I done gone too far now to have to start lying to my own self, too. He was there all right. It was Judge Long. That's why we came."

"With Jula Mae?" Jefferson asked.

Newt nodded.

They rode back down the dark road and the sweat on Newt's back cooled and made him shiver. "Be a good night for a drink if there is such a thing."

Jefferson looked at the boy out of the corner of his eye, waiting for him to continue.

"Sometimes I wonder if dreaming about something good that happens ain't really better than the thing itself happening. I mean, once you've dreamed about it, it's like it's already been done and then when that thing actually happens it don't seem as special as it was when you was just hoping for it to happen."

After a long, thoughtful pause, the boy turned to Jefferson, "You think you could work folks, Jefferson?"

"What folks?"

"Take a crew out and be in charge over folks out in the woods, getting all the timber cut and back to the mill, telling 'em what to do and how to do it and all?"

"I ain't never been boss on nobody. But I reckon I could get done what all you just said."

"If you could take care of that end, I reckon I could learn to take care of the rest of it, the figuring and all."

Jefferson gave an almost imperceptible nod.

"How many acres you and Ida been sharecropping for Papa?" Newt asked.

"They's 'bout twenty in that one field."

"How many acres in that old Tarver place where you and Ida stay, that whole place, the homeplace, the fields, that patch of woods, everything?"

"'Bout fo'ty what I always heard."

"You reckon you're gonna want to fool with that whiskey business after that dream?"

"Preacher say colored folks is too afraid of things to get what white folks got. I ain't like that no more. Folks is gonna have 'em they whiskey. I ain't gonna drink it no more, but I can't say for sure 'bout selling it."

"I was reading in the back of a magazine that said you could make good money growing what they called ginseng in the hills," Newt said. "It says them Chinese people'll pay a high price for it. It's got a place you can write off to and find out everything about it. That'd have to be legal. It being in a magazine and all."

"I just wants me some land," Jefferson said.

"My granddaddy, the one that left me the gold watch, used to say, 'Put all your money into land and something good's bound to happen.' He always said that's why folks come here in the first place, all the way across the ocean, just to have 'em a piece of land. I don't reckon you could go wrong putting your money in the one thing all them folks came so far to get in the first place. Wouldn't it be something if we up and bought a bunch of land and it all started with risking that gold watch of my granddaddy's? If we was to work the whiskey business for another year or two, Lord have mercy, we could sure have some money to buy some land. Look what we done already made. Hap's already working on getting us a good piece of land, and we ain't even hardly got started good yet."

"Some folks just knows they won't never get 'em no land. Drinking helps 'em ease they pain."

CHAPTER 24

At daybreak on the seventh and final day of the trial, Newt followed the deputy down the long hall to see his father. They walked past the open door of Earl's cell, and Newt saw that the sheets were bunched at the foot of his father's cot, the pillow on the floor. The deputy led him into a room at the end of the hall where Earl sat behind a wooden table, Mr. Upchurch standing at his side. The boy masked the grimace of a slight limp as he entered the room cradling a large brown envelope.

Upchurch stood rigidly, his arms folded and head held high to stretch into his proper height. But despite the attorney's effort to maintain a stiff presence, his expression soon hinted that he recognized something pleasing in the boy's nature, though Newt had yet to speak a word. He broke out of his formal pose and moved toward the boy, his hand extended. "I'm Howard Upchurch." Newt shook his hand, giving a polite but cautious nod.

"Please," Upchurch said. "Have a seat." Newt sat across from his father and placed the envelope on the table without taking his fingers from its edges. As the boy sat down, Earl exhaled a moan from deep within, a soft bawl of anguish escaping his insides with neither warning nor apparent control. He ran both hands over his thin and matted hair and then clasped them in front of his face with his elbows on the table. He followed the movement of Newt's fingers on the corners of the envelope through his bulbous eyes.

Mr. Upchurch broke the silence. "Your father tells me that you might have some information, some insight that may be beneficial to our case."

Newt shifted in his seat and nodded, still silent.

Upchurch leaned across the table and removed his glasses. "Young man, do you know that I could subpoena you as a witness?"

"Yes sir. If you say you could, then I ain't got no reason to think you can't. I don't know all that much about the law."

"Do you still believe you can deliver on the deal you proposed to your father several weeks ago?"

Newt glanced quickly at his father, then back at Upchurch. "Yes sir. I still believe it."

"Then either you know something about the facts of this case that you are withholding from us, or you know something about this jury that we ought to know." He lifted the gold watch from his vest pocket and let it settle in his hand as he spoke. "In less than two hours from now your father's future will be out of our hands and into the hands of the twelve people on that jury. I'd like to give you a chance to do the right thing, son. What is it you know?"

Newt did not see it coming. He only sensed the sudden stirring of motion, his father rising, and then the streak of balled fist and forearm that was on him before he could focus on it, the sudden impact catching him behind the ear and knocking him off the chair onto the floor. With his hands and face against the cool concrete floor, he watched the shuffling of feet and heard the rise of the familiar spit-inflected voice boiling through the muted ringing in his ears. "Tell us what you know, you little piss-ant bastard! Tell us what you know!"

Newt picked up the envelope off the floor and sat back down, placing his palm gently on top of it as if he were feeling for the pulse of a small animal. Upchurch stood up and worked Earl slowly into the corner. Newt could not hear the words, but

Upchurch's tone was composed, finally pulling Earl's raging eyes off the boy.

They returned to the table, and Earl sat down with Upchurch standing behind him, keeping his hand firmly on Earl's shoulder. "The last time you came to visit your father, you said, 'I know a way to get you out of here.' This morning, you tell us that you can still deliver on that promise. I've been practicing criminal law for twenty-six years, young man, and it's hard for me to believe that you can possibly know anything, much less do anything, that would set your father free. But your father is the one that will have to live with this decision, and he has instructed me to accept the arrangement you've proposed, with one caveat."

Newt opened the envelope and set the documents on the table between them. "Once he signs all these, I'll finish doing what needs to be done."

"Who prepared these documents for you?" Upchurch asked.

"A friend of mind who knows the law. I don't guess it really matters who. It's just what I told him it'd be," Newt said, tilting his head slightly toward his father without looking at him.

"What if you can't do what you promise to do, son?" Upchurch asked.

Newt looked down toward the gold watch now lying on the table. "I reckon we'll all find out soon enough."

"You did not ask about the caveat that I added to your proposal. You don't care to hear it?" Upchurch asked.

"I thought that was just a fancy way of saying you was taking the deal."

"Your father and I think it would be best for us to hold these documents until you complete your end of the bargain."

Again, Newt placed his right palm lightly over the documents before he spoke. "No sir. I'll feel better if I just hold on to 'em. If I don't do what I say I can, then I'll give 'em back to y'all and you can tear 'em up. You got my word on it."

Mr. Upchurch sat down and leaned forward toward the boy again. "If this plan of yours doesn't work out, and you don't bring these documents back to me at the end of the trial, I'll have you arrested on charges of extortion. Are you sure you know what that means, son?"

Newt did not answer, resting his eyes on the papers before him.

Upchurch read through the documents as he handed them over one by one for Earl Ham to sign. When he had finished, Earl pushed the stack of papers toward the boy, holding his hand on them to make the boy look into his eyes before he released them. Earl stared into his son's eyes for several seconds before he spoke. "Ain't no way no little chicken-shit bastard like you is my own flesh and blood. You worse than that slobbering-ass brother of yours. You better make damn sure you do deliver, boy. If you don't get me outta here, I'll have somebody come and find you. If they is a God, boy, you better pray to Him that don't happen."

Newt put the papers back in the envelope and stood up, looking at Upchurch. "Before the judge instructs the jury, you ask for this." Newt handed him the piece of paper with the words written on it.

Upchurch took the paper and read it out loud. "Motion for a directed verdict of acquittal."

"You mean that's it? That's all you got?" Upchurch asked.

"Yes sir, that's all you'll need."

Upchurch followed Newt into the hall and gripped his arm tightly as he spoke. "Son, if you know something about this case that we need to know I'd strongly advise you to tell me here and now. Withholding evidence from a court of law is a criminal offense. You could go to jail for a long time. You know what they'll do to a pretty young boy like you in there? Do you, boy?"

Newt walked out of Upchurch's hold and turned around. "Just ask for what's on that piece of paper."

Dawn was beginning to break as Newt crawled into the office through the window. He sat in a corner chair and watched the first light narrow through the curtain and angle like a long dagger across the bookcases. He thought of McAllister's office and felt comfort in being surrounded by so many books, in the hope that perhaps people did care enough about the law, about justice itself to fill the pages of so many books with it. There was comfort, too, in the certainty that today it would be over, that in the hours ahead the future would unfold and appear in front of him like a green meadow out of a creek bottom that he had never seen before, had never imagined existed.

The judge entered his chambers and did not sense Newt sitting in the chair in the corner. He hung his tweed jacket over the back of his chair and sat down at his desk. Newt looked beyond the burly eyebrows and high forehead, studying the closed mouth and round jaw for a hint of how the hollowness of jaw, the gumming of what had looked to be a toothless mouth, had worked that night at Jula Mae's.

Newt's voice did not seem sudden; it lifted smoothly into the room in no more than a whisper, as if it were sifted from the silence itself. "That's one bad dog she's got, ain't it?"

The judge gathered the image of the boy into focus without flinching, as if he had known a voice would rise there, as if he knew the shadows well enough to be at home in what stirred from them. The judge opened the drawer to his desk without looking down and reached his hand inside. "You Earl Ham's boy, ain't you?"

Newt moved out of the shadowed corner and took a seat in front of the judge's desk. "I sure hope I didn't scare you bad."

"What you better hope is you got a goddamn good reason for being in my chambers, boy."

"The fact is, Judge, I ain't got no choice but to be here. The fact is, I'd rather be anyplace else."

"Bad dog?" the judge snapped.

"Yes sir. That dog of Jula Mae's. That rascal got to be part wolf. But I reckon y'all heard it all y'allselves. Y'all probably thought it was a coon or a possum, but it was me. Had me treed up a cedar tree. Took a little hide off my leg too, while he was getting it done."

The judge closed the drawer to the desk and leaned back in his chair as if he were trying to place the boy, trying to reconcile the youth with the words, the innocent yet determined face with the clumsy sire. "You the one left that note on the windshield."

"Yes sir. I didn't mean no disrespect, Judge. I done seen that old black car of yours parked behind that shed every Saturday night we've come through Berner, and then I seen that same old car parked up at the courthouse in that spot that says it's reserved for you. I done heard that Jula Mae sells it from time to time and I just put it all together. Only thing left was to just see for myself."

"You got a point you heading to, boy, or you just running for something, making a speech?"

"I done been over what I got to say in my head about a hundred times, Judge. But I can't figure no way to say it that's gonna make it any easier on you to hear. This morning, in your courtroom, my papa's lawyer is gonna make a motion for a directed verdict of acquittal. If you'll give a verdict of not guilty, then you got my word I won't never say nothing about what I seen. Now they ain't much my papa won't do or ain't done. But I can tell you, Judge, he didn't kill that deputy. You ain't gotta worry about that. If you do let him off, you won't never have to let your conscience worry you."

Judge Long clasped his hands behind his neck and reared his head back, looking at Newt down the crook of his nose and smiling. "Conscience? Goddamn boy. Conscience ain't got nothing to do with the law. Justice ain't wrote nowhere in these books. Hell. Ain't no justice but what I call justice."

"Yes sir," Newt said. "I reckon that's why I'm here."

"Boy, what's to keep me from calling the sheriff in here right now and throwing you in jail with your papa on the charge of obstructing justice, trying to intimidate a judge?"

"Yes sir. You could do that, throw me in jail. I can't even say I'd blame you if you did. But don't you reckon that all them people out there'll be wanting to know what it was I was obstructing you about?"

"What's to make you think I give a shit if you tell everybody in the county? Ain't no law against a white man visiting a colored gal."

"I ain't saying you'd get in no legal trouble, but if I was to step out on them front steps and tell all the folks about what I saw, show 'em how you was working them gums and standing and all, that'd be a lot for 'em to be talking about."

"It'll be my word against yours boy, and I'm a judge. Who you think them folks is gonna believe?"

"Well sir. That's true what you say about more of 'em might believe you than me, but I suspect all of 'em will be doing a heap of wondering about it from here on out. I sure don't mean no disrespect, Judge. People say you're a good man. Some say your wife is the nicest lady to ever set foot in this county."

"Get your ass out of here, boy." The judge swiveled his chair around with his back toward Newt, staring out the window at the crowd starting to gather on the courthouse lawn.

"All rise. The Superior Court of Butts County is now in session. The Honorable Judge Horatio Long, presiding." The judge looked pale but resolute as he sat down, the black robe providing enough dignity to his presence to allow for the bushy brows, the hollow jaw. He stared over his half glasses directly at Newt as if to measure the boy's nerve in the crowded room, the way a man holds his finger on his queen before moving it, looking at his chess opponent one final time to measure the danger of releasing it. The boy returned the look with a distant resignation and the weary calm that strains the fear out of inevitability.

Mr. Upchurch rose. "Permission to approach the bench, Your Honor."

"All right," the judge said. "Approach."

Upchurch and the prosecutor came around to the side of the bench. "Your Honor," Upchurch started, "I have a motion to make outside the presence of the jury."

"I object," the prosecutor said. "With all due respect, Your Honor, this is just a desperate move on the part of a desperate man. It's time to instruct the jury, Your Honor. We've had six long days of testimony. It's time for the jury to decide this case."

The judge turned from the men and scanned the soft whispers of the courtroom. He took off his glasses and looked the prosecutor in the eye. "Overruled. I'll hear the motion." The judge turned toward the jury. "The jury is dismissed. Bailiff, take the jury to the waiting room until I call 'em back."

The murmur in the courtroom rose to the heightened pitch of cicada wailing toward the final blink of twilight. The judge slammed his gavel down. "I'll have order in this court, or I'll clear this courtroom out."

Mr. Upchurch stood in front of the defense table. "Your Honor, after hearing the testimony in this case, I am compelled, on behalf of my client, to move for a directed verdict of acquittal. The fact is, the prosecution has failed to prove their case. Not only has the prosecution failed to produce any eyewitnesses to the crime, they have offered no concrete evidence whatsoever that my client killed the deputy. With all due respect, Your Honor, where's the motive? The prosecution has conveniently circumvented any discussion of motive for one reason and one reason alone: there simply is no motive in this case. My client is a well-respected businessman in this community. There is no sane reason why he would kill anyone, much less an officer of the law. The prosecution has said that they have the murder weapon. But, Your Honor, the prosecution has been unable to explain why there were two spent cartridges in the pistol and, furthermore, they have been unable to find the bullet that killed the deputy. Therefore, we have no way of knowing that the shot that killed the deputy came from my client's gun. Your Honor, I respectfully submit to this court that the evidence in this case demands a verdict of not guilty. I make a motion for a directed verdict of acquittal."

The prosecutor stood up in front of his table. "Your Honor, what we've got here is nothing more than a last-ditch ploy of a man running scared. And we all know why he's running scared, don't we? He knows we've proved beyond a shadow of a doubt his client's guilt. Your Honor, this man's a known moonshiner. What do folks who are in the moonshine business do? Why, they murder folks that get in their way. This case has got the oldest motive known to man, Your Honor, and that's greed, pure and simple. Your Honor, we don't need to recover the bullet that murdered Eugene Raintree to prove guilt. The sheriff of this county came on the scene of the crime five minutes after it happened with the murder weapon lying at the defendant's feet. There is no ghost murderer in this case. I ask your honor to deny the motion for directed verdict. Let the jury decide, Your Honor. Let the people decide."

Judge Long had listened intently as the prosecutor spoke. As Whatley sat down, the judge sighed gently before he spoke. "There'll be a fifteen-minute recess, and I'll return with my decision."

Newt looked across the courtroom at Sheriff Wills sitting with the Raintree family—the mother, two brothers, and one sister. The mother was small and wiry, hard around the edges with sharp, time-defying features, her gray hair pulled tight behind her head and the brave hat, flowered and faded, pulled down on her forehead the same way a man wears his hat to keep the sun off his eyes in the field. Her figure was too narrow for Newt to imagine that she could have birthed an animal the size of Eugene and much less the son by her side who had the same overbite, the same stuck lip on the tooth as if the lip itself was made too small to cover it. The daughter's hatless hair, light as an albino mare, faded into her white eyebrows and white lips, the dull gray eyes, close-set and mute, wandered across the walls and ceiling of the courtroom to settle into her lap. The younger brother looked to be about Newt's age. He sat next to his sister, perfectly relaxed and at ease with the proceeding, working an almost imperceptible plug of tobacco from one side of his jaw to the other when he felt no one was looking. As if he had sensed someone's eyes were on him, he looked across the room to find Newt staring at him, and he acknowledged the stare with a slight grin through his cheek and eyes without so much as moving his lips. The whole family soon followed the boy's stare toward Newt the way a pack of coyotes does when one in the pack stands too still and stares too long in one direction.

"All rise." The judge sat down and leaned forward, clasping his hands together. He looked neither to the prosecutor nor the defendant, but straight down the aisle of the courtroom toward the heavy oak doors. "For seven days now I have listened to the testimony of this trial, a trial that seeks to bring justice to the death of a young man who came to our community to serve as an officer of the law, a young man who was killed in the line of duty. The prosecution has presented a convincing theory of how Deputy Raintree was killed. A man of unquestioned integrity, Sheriff Wills, has testified that he arrived on the scene of the crime not more than five minutes after he heard a shot fired and found the deputy dead and the defendant within a few feet of him, a gun lying by his side, two bullets spent from the chamber. What we have seen unfold before us in the last seven days is, as the prosecution has stated, a simple study of greed, the symptoms of which beget a craving like the very moonshine whiskey the defendant admits he sells, breeding by its very nature the uncontrollable desire for more. There is little doubt in my mind that the defendant here today is a product of that greed and has little, if any, regard for the laws of this great state.

"But the defendant is not on trial here today for selling illegal moonshine whiskey. He is on trial for the murder of Eugene Raintree, second-degree murder. In order to uphold the office that I was elected to by the people of this circuit and perform my duties in strict accordance with the laws of the State of Georgia, I must declare that the evidence in this trial, taken with all reasonable deductions and inferences from that evidence, demands a verdict of not guilty. Therefore, I direct a verdict of acquittal for the defendant. Mr. Ham, you are free to go. Bailiff, tell the jury they are dismissed. Court is adjourned."

Newt watched Eugene's mother rise as the judge declared the verdict. She placed her hands flat on the rail in front of her as if she were on her own front porch squinting at the twisted corn in the field, readying herself to spit her snuff clean from her mouth and curse the rainless sky to where it broke into heaven itself. Her boys and girl rose up beside her, the older son leaning forward toward the embrace of Upchurch and Earl Ham, lip caught on tooth again in the effortless snarl with the tongue reaching up to moisten the out-of-reach lip. His face held the puzzled look of one coming to a hog pen and seeing the fence down and no hog, just the broken rail and the tracks leading through the woods. The woman turned and walked the very corridor down which the judge's words had echoed. The children followed their mother out, walking behind her like chicks behind a game hen, scattered but swept in the current of her movement.

The Raintrees waited at the oak tree on the front lawn of the courthouse until the sheriff approached them, his gun back on, the high, thick waist pivoting over his hips. Newt stood beside the steps and watched the woman's sharp finger point once at the sheriff and once back at the building. He could not distinguish her words, only the urgent twang of her speech. The oldest son stood slightly bent, head toward the ground, leaning into the voices of his mother and the sheriff with the impenetrable ear of a man who listens not to the meanings of the words but only to their sound because he knows already what will be asked, what will be instructed. With his thumbs jammed into his pockets, he waited for the last word uttered, the final phrase, like the bell to a fighter that would set him into motion. The youngest brother stood relaxed in the sunlight, his delicate and handsome face as out of place within the family as a thoroughbred colt born into a herd of draft horses. He caught Newt's stare again. Brushing one finger across the brim of his hat, he winked.

Newt walked to the truck where Jefferson watched his hurried gait as the boy angled across the lawn toward him. He hopped in the truck and pointed to Redbone. "We better get to the house in case Papa decides to come straight there."

CHAPTER 25

During the week following the trial, the news spread like wind-blown lint from freshly picked cotton, finding its way into every tilted shack and low-branch gully, outpacing the hill farmers, their wives, and children riding on wagons down the river road, and even the old trucks that rattled and sputtered past them. The talk, the speculation of the outcome of the trial, the verdict and what it meant to each of them, was suddenly rendered barren by the discovery the morning after. Earl Ham's familiar truck was found in the river, one taillight shining like a sturgeon's eye in the stained orange water, a direct and motionless verdict in its own right.

On Saturday morning most of the folks within riding distance of Redbone headed toward Mr. Bludie's store, moving the excitement of the trial to a new location like gypsies following the scent of sawdust and elephants. They leaned their heads into the wind, trailing the ripening hope of a miraculous mathematics, the possibility that the river itself, the very river that they lived on and in all likelihood would die on, had washed their debts clean.

Hap, the mule trader, trailed behind the crowd from Berner to Redbone more out of reflex than deliberation, swept up by the draft of something akin to a red and dust-ridden land rush and driven by his own intuitive sense to supply the demand it created. He had come to the trial at Berner pulling the same black-and-tan coon dog on the same frayed plowline, and he made his way into Redbone that morning on a buckboard pulled by a fiddle-headed blue-roan mule, the coon dog now sitting by his side on the seat, its jowls open, smiling luxuriously into the breeze. Hap pulled his wagon around the back and strolled in his urgent and sinewy gait toward the crowd gathered in front of the store, dragging the slew-footed dog behind him.

"Here he is, boys," he said loudly. "The Hanging Judge is what I call him. 'Cause when that 'un there strikes a coon track it ain't long 'fore that ringtail is caught and hung up to skin. This here dog's so doggone fast that when he gets to running, it looks like nary a one of them feets is hitting the ground. But look here now, if that name don't suit you, boys, he'll come to most anything. Last man what owned him called him Cash, 'cause he bought him a little piece of bottom land off'n all the hides this young hound delivered to him."

"I thought you done sold that dog to a man up at the Berner trial," one man said.

"Hey," another cried out. "Ain't you the man what owned that chimp that got its ass whupped here a while back?"

Hap's pointed white hat bobbed matter-of-factly as he addressed the first man who had spoken. "I done that, neighbor, just what you said. I traded him for that old smart-headed roan mule over there and the wagon that goes behind her. Got out traded a little, I reckon, but who's counting? If you can't give a good deal every now and then to a neighbor, then who can you give a good deal to, neighbor?" Hap turned to the second man, a hint of bitterness in his eye. "And yes sir, I am the man what owned that chimp, old Abe was his name, God rest his soul, what got his self whupped here a while back like you just give witness to."

"What you still got that same hound for is what I'm asking?" the first man said.

"Well sir. That young man what I traded him to got his self in a little tight right up there at the trial goings on. Yes sir. He got to rolling them bones with what I figured to be a pretty rough set of folks. They had all done got right whiskey-headed by the time I

That Mr. Freeman done a fine job on Earl, though, getting his
color back after being in that river all night. You couldn't even see
that hole in his forehead the way they had his hair all brushed
down on it. I don't reckon they had to worry with covering up
that other hole."

"Which other'n?" the woman asked.

"The one below his waist, honey. You ain't heard? Had one
between his eyes and one twixt his legs." Mrs. Bludie leaned into
the woman's ear and whispered. "Mr. Freeman's wife told me they
just trimmed off what was left of it."

"Well I never!" The woman moved her hand from her neck
to cover her mouth and then craned her thick neck around again
to find the black girl easing quietly down the aisle, holding a
forefinger to her white teeth.

"Mr. Freeman sure does a fine job on them that's passed,
don't he?" Mrs. Bludie repeated.

"Yes'm. I reckon he does. What'd the preacher have to say
over Earl?"

"Preacher? Wasn't no preacher there, honey. Miss Naomi
wouldn't allow it, so they say."

"You mean they just lowered him on in the ground without
nobody saying a thing?"

"No ma'am. Newt got up and said a few words."

"Little Newt got up and said something? Bless his heart."

"You should of heard him, too. I don't even think his mama
knew he was to say anything. She sure didn't look it when he got
up."

"What'd he say?"

"Was more like a little old prayer than anything else."

"Was?"

"Yes ma'am."

"What'd that sweet child say?"

"Well, let me see now if I can remember it like he done it. 'Lord,' he said, 'don't nobody down here know Papa better'n we do, and I know if we can forgive him then surely it won't be no trouble for You to. And Lord, if You'll be so kind as to take him on with You now and not count every last thing he done against him, we give you our word we'll work real hard, do our best to fix up most of the wrong he done while he was down here.' Then he picked up a handful of dirt and sprinkled it over the casket."

"Lord God. That was it?"

"No ma'am. Then it got real quiet for the longest time and all of a sudden Ida went over and stood by Naomi."

"Ida?"

"Yes ma'am. She walked over and stood shoulder to shoulder with Naomi and started singing 'Amazin' Grace.'"

"Sister, I reckon it *would* have to be amazing to cover that man," the woman said. "Lord, Lord, would you listen to me? Ida sure can sing, can't she?"

"Like an angel."

CHAPTER 26

Newt steered the small boat down the edge of the riverbank. The sun was warm on their shoulders though there would be little left of it. Addie sat in the bottom of the boat twisting a rope around his hand, his eyes wandering from bank to bank to watch a turtle slide off a rock or a gar turn a ripple in the water. Newt balanced the oar over his knees and let the steady current drift them quietly southwards. Down river, an osprey shrilled at the intrusion, circled twice at a safe distance, then lit in a large pine on the edge of the riverbank.

"You know we could just keep right on going," Newt said. "They say this river goes all the way to the ocean. We could kill squirrels along the way and catch fish and cook 'em. But I don't reckon you'd care too much for me killing those squirrels, would you? I can't say I blame you. I ain't so sure I ever want to see a gun again.

"Who knows? When we get to the end of this river, we might even find a ship to take up with and go all the way around the world. We've got more than enough to make a new start somewhere. There ain't no telling what this bag of silver is really worth. Maybe one day we'd end up down in Argentina and find the boy whose papa owned this silver. That'd be something, wouldn't it? To settle up with him." Addie remained still, hushed as if in a temple, floating through a strange land.

The current began to drift the boat sideways, and Newt dug the oar behind the boat to set it straight, making a hollow thump that echoed up the river. Addie craned his neck around to follow the sound until it faded out of hearing, then looked up, jaw loose with a question. Newt hooked his arm playfully around Addie's neck and pulled him closer. "It's all right. I won't let nothing get you."

The river widened before them, and Newt looked from bank to bank to measure its width. "That was sure some dream Jefferson had about crossing the river in a ship where they took him to a better place. I reckon there was a reason I wasn't in that dream. I would of liked to have been there, though. I guess this old boat is our ship, and we'll just have to do the steering the best we can."

He paddled three or four smooth strokes into the water, and the boat steadied. The shoals around the next bend hissed in the distance like grain sifting from the sky. Newt spoke softly, within the comfort of their silence. "I can't help it. I just can't keep from wondering why Mama never told me. I've always had this feeling, for as long as I can remember, that something wasn't like it was supposed to be. Sometimes I let myself forget about it, figuring that maybe some folks were just born to be sad and suffer more'n others. But I guess now she's got what she been wanting all along. McAllister's a good man. He must be if Mama's loved him all these years. But somehow it still don't feel right.

"When I first came to realize that you were Earl's only son, it scared me. It made me feel like you was even more alone in this world, since you was having to carry all the bad with me not carrying my share anymore. I ain't never told you this before, but sometimes when he'd whip you with that strap, and you never would show any meanness or bawl like he wanted you to, I could see something in his eyes, almost like he was a little proud somehow about the way you could take a beating. Mama never loved him so that means he died without nobody loving him. I ain't aiming to die that way. I've studied on it a good bit. Earl must've known all along that I wasn't his son. That's bound to be hard on any man."

The river was straight for a long stretch then curved into the mound that rose like a serpent's head into the horizon, and they navigated its sleek body, the sharpness of the November sun rippling the water like the fine scales of its back. "There it is," the boy said, pointing ahead. "Everybody says these mounds are haunted, have spirits in 'em. I've heard stories about people seeing ghosts and hearing strange sounds up here. There's supposed to be warriors' and chiefs' skulls up there. I don't know why, but ghosts don't hardly seem worth worrying about anymore. I'd be a lot more scared of some of the things I done found out are real than them that just could be. Most folks won't even go up there, especially after dark. That silver'll be safe up there for as long as we want it to be."

Newt pulled the boat through the willow branches and tied it. He helped Addie out of the boat and lifted the heavy bag of silver over his shoulder. They walked through the giant silver-barked sycamores along the riverbank until they came to the head of a path that led up to the mounds. Halfway up the trail, Newt stopped and let the bag of silver drop to his feet. He looked up the trunk of a white oak that was the largest he had ever seen. "Reckon how they missed that one," he said, looking up into its crown. "There's lots of lumber in that tree. It's already dropping acorns, too. It'll feed lots of deer and coon." He leaned against the tree and looked down the river. "This tree's old enough to have had many an Indian lean against it and look down this river just like I'm doing." He turned to address his brother. "I wonder what they thought when they saw the first white man coming up that river. They probably didn't know enough meanness to think bad of it at first." He snapped his fingers. "Now they're all in Oklahoma somewheres. I'll bet they ain't got no trees like this out there. They found out soon enough; folks around here won't let nothing stand in the way of getting what they want. Just think about it. Those Indians had all this for free. They probably figured all along God give it to 'em. I don't imagine they ever dreamed He would take it away. Now folks'll do whatever it takes to get it."

He turned to Addie, who had leaned against the tree beside him. "Except for you, Addie," he tousled his brother's hair. "You ain't even got enough meanness in you to put a worm on a hook. I guess we're different in that way. There were things that I wanted, things that I thought had to be done, and I never really saw meanness come into it till it was way too late."

Addie picked at the wildflowers as they reached the crest of the mound. Newt found a small cedar tree and dropped the bag of silver by it. He took out a piece of a broken plow shank and started digging. Addie sat down beside him and watched Newt's pace gain momentum as he dug the dark earth into his lap, the profile of his grandfather's felt fedora pulled down over the tops of his ears, making him look like an old man prodding at his own grave. He raised the shank higher and higher as he thrust it into the earth, speaking within the rhythm of his digging. "If I just hadn't snapped that twig—or seen where Earl buried that man—none of this would of happened." He stopped and turned to Addie, sensing what the words he had just spoken must have sounded like to the boy. His voice was now calm, reassuring. "It had to be done, Addie. He never would of done what he said he'd do."

He dug faster and faster and deeper and deeper until the taste came to him again, the deep-bile bitterness that had first come to him as a young boy when his fever had risen out of control and wild-colored creatures danced and taunted him from the corners of his room. Only this time the taste came quickly and moved so far down into the recesses of his throat that he was afraid he would never be able to spit it out, rid himself of it. With it came new

images and sounds, though no less fearsome than the
hallucinations of his fever: the report like a single limb cracking in
an ice storm, and the deputy's face, cheek tight with tobacco and
eyes suspended in the crosswinds of disbelief. And then looking
upward, as if waiting for the sky to sound, he dropped the shank to
listen for the shot by the river, no less heard yet as far reaching as
the slow tentacles of summer thunder. He fell to his back and
looked into the starlit night, his breathing heavy, uneven.

Every depth and crevice of the western sky unfolded into the
boy's eyes, a thousand flickering pine knots outlining the path into
a great bayou. The stars seemed so bright that, although he knew
them to be millions of miles away, for a moment he believed he
could feel their warmth on his damp forehead. "We'll just have to
give away everything that's given to us from now on. We'll start
with this silver."

A thin dark cloud slid into the moon like coal smoke parting
the rib bone of a small animal. He found Orion's belt and there,
he imagined the great sword, unsheathed and poised in
magnificent hands above him, searching for the glint of his eye as
it peeped from the tangled briars of the earth. Then, he and Addie
saw it at the same time, the long shooting star that arched down
like a feather burning to its quill. Addie pointed toward the traces
of purple and blue that the falling star had left, and snuggling into
Newt's shoulder he cooed once, then twisted his lips with
forefinger and thumb as if to pull a word from them. The sound
was drawling, like the first bawl of a newborn lamb: "Paaa…."

Newt rose to his knees and looked into his brother's eyes, and
there he saw it for the second time, within the troubled mouth
and heavy brow was the gaze of a prophet at perfect ease with the
depths of time.